DATE DUE			

BOOKS BY ROBERT NEWMAN

The Boy Who Could Fly
The Japanese
Merlin's Mistake
The Testing of Tertius
The Shattered Stone
Night Spell
The Case of the Baker Street Irregular
The Case of the Vanishing Corpse
The Case of the Somerville Secret
The Case of the Threatened King
The Case of the Etruscan Treasure
The Case of the Frightened Friend
The Case of the Murdered Players
The Case of the Indian Curse
The Case of the Watching Boy

The Case of
the Watching
Boy

The Case of the Watching Boy

by Robert Newman

A JEAN KARL BOOK

Atheneum 1987 *New York*

Atheneum
Macmillan Publishing Company
866 Third Avenue, New York, NY 10022
Collier Macmillan Canada, Inc.

Type set by Maryland Linotype, Baltimore, Maryland
Printed and bound by Fairfield Graphics, Fairfield, Pennsylvania
Designed by Mary Ahern
First Edition

10 9 8 7 6 5 4 3 2 1

Library of Congress Cataloging-in-Publication Data

Newman, Robert,
The case of the watching boy.

"A Jean Karl book."
SUMMARY: Two English schoolboys inadvertently
become involved in a kidnapping which strangely connects
with the succession to the throne of Rumania.
[1. Mystery and detective stories] I. Title.
PZ7.4857Cav   1987   [Fic]   86-28859
ISBN 0-689-31317-9

Contents

1. An Official Request 3
2. The Watcher on the Tor 8
3. The Knights Errant 22
4. Disaster! 30
5. Enter the Inspector 39
6. The Gypsies 53
7. Coral 60
8. The Coachman 73
9. The Embassy 87
10. The Colonel Is Outraged 104
11. The Foreign Office Is Concerned ... 114
12. The Yard's Junior Branch 127
13. Inside the Embassy 135
14. Jasper Again 145
15. Reunion 153
16. A Royal Explanation 160

The Case of the Watching Boy

1

An Official Request

"Ah, there you are," said the headmaster as Andrew opened the door of his study. "Come in, my boy, and sit down." He studied Andrew through his gold-rimmed spectacles as he sat down on the other side of the large desk. "Surprised that I sent for you?"

"A bit, sir."

"But it didn't worry you?"

"No, sir."

"Good. I commended you on that the last time I asked you to come see me, said it was proof of a clear conscience. And I'm delighted that your conscience remains as limpid as ever. The fact is that I asked you to come here because I wanted to ask you if you would do me—and the school—a service."

"If I can, sir, I'll be happy to."

"Oh, you can—there's no question about that. Whether

you'll want to is something else again. But the only way
we can determine that is for me to tell you what I want.
Do you know Markham? Christopher Markham?"

"Yes, sir. I do."

"What do you know about him?"

"Well, he's a little younger than I am—about a year.
And he's not in my house, so I don't know him as well
as I do many other chaps, but he's a fairly good cricketer,
a very good tennis player, and on the whole, quite well
liked. But with it all, he's something of a solitary."

"Yes, he is. Do you know anything about his family?"

"No, sir. I heard he's an orphan."

"Not quite. His mother's dead, died shortly after he
was born. But his father's alive, attached to our embassy
in Peking at the moment. He has no close relatives, so
he stays with Mrs. Bartram and me during holidays. That
gives me a rather special responsibility as far as he's concerned."

"Yes, I can see that, sir."

"Mr. Slyke, his housemaster, was here to see me last
night. He's a little worried about Markham, and he got
me worried." He paused. "What did you mean when you
said he was something of a solitary?"

"Well, he does like to walk alone, sir. I don't mean
that as a figure of speech. He seems to have some fairly
good friends. But he also does like to go off alone, walk
the Downs, collect mineral specimens, and watch birds."

"How do you know?"

4

"Because I've met him out on the Downs."

"In other words, you like to walk alone, too."

"Sometimes. Yes, sir."

"Of course I knew that. That's one of the reasons I wanted to talk to you. The reason Mr. Slyke is worried about Markham is not because he's been going off alone almost every afternoon recently—but because he suspects he's been slipping off at night and coming back just before dawn."

"I see, sir."

"That's why I called you in. To ask you whether you'd be willing to look into the matter for me." Andrew glanced at him, then down. "Well?"

"If you don't mind, sir, I'd rather not."

"Why not?"

"Because its seems to me it's a kind of sneaking."

"When you say sneaking you mean spying, informing. Or, in the vernacular, peaching, snitching, or squealing."

"Yes, sir."

"In one respect, that's the sort of answer I'd expect from you. In another, it not only saddens me—it shocks me. How long have you been here at Medford?"

"Three years, sir."

"In all that time have I ever done or said anything that would suggest that I would—not just encourage or approve—but even *tolerate* sneaking?"

"No, sir."

"Have any of the masters?"

"No, sir."

"Then how could you imply that that was what I was asking you to do?"

"Sir, I apologize. But the truth is that there are schools where it *is* encouraged."

"So I've heard. But I wouldn't have anyone here—boy or master—who would be capable of such a thing. When I asked if you would look into this matter of Markham's behavior, I meant just that. I don't want you to tell me what he's been up to. Since he's alone here and I'm acting *in loco parentis*, I would merely like to know if he's involved in anything I should be concerned about."

"I see, sir. One more question. Why are you asking me to do this?"

"An interesting question. You happen to be one of the best-liked boys in school. Not just because you play a good game of cricket or because you're pleasant, honest and—I understand—intelligent and amusing. But because of what is believed about you."

"Believed?"

"Yes. Your mother is a well-known actress. You never talk about her. Your stepfather is with Scotland Yard. You never talk about him either. But the fact that you haven't has encouraged the boys here to imagine a very rich life for you in which—during holidays—you meet many of England's famous actresses who are friends of your mother's. And even more interesting and exciting, you help your stepfather solve his most difficult cases."

"I see. It's true that I don't talk about my mother or stepfather—any more than Chadwick talks about his father, who is in the Foreign Office, or Dunwoodie, whose father is a general—but that's the only part of what you've said that's true."

"Is that so? I've heard rumors that lead me to believe there's a modicum of truth in what they believe. But that's beside the point. The boys will continue to believe what they want to believe and you must suffer the consequences. This is one of them. I trust you and I believe that Markham does, too. That's why I made the request of you that I did. The question is, will you do what I've asked you to do? Will you—being as open as you like—cast a friendly eye on Markham?"

Again Andrew hesitated a moment. Then he nodded. "Yes, sir. I will."

2

The Watcher on the Tor

It was by sheer good luck that Andrew found Markham as soon as he did. After Latin, his last class of the day, he walked over to St. Edmund's, Markham's house. There was no sign of him in the quad, at the fives court, or on the playing field where two house cricket teams were practicing. That meant he was probably out on the Downs, but where? After all, they extended in every direction for miles around the school. The last time Andrew had met him on the Downs it had been near the foot of Bodmin's Tor, which lay northwest of the school.

He looked toward the tor, about three-quarters of a mile from the school, and there, at the top of it, he saw a sudden flash as something bright reflected the westering sun. Was it Markham? It might be. Even if it wasn't, the tor was a good place to look over the Downs, see if he was elsewhere.

It took about a half hour to walk to the tor and climb the steep, rocky southern face. When Andrew got to the top, he saw that his guess had been a good one. There was Markham, stretched out with a pair of field glasses beside him.

"Hello," he said quietly and without surprise. He had apparently been watching Andrew approach through the glasses, and it had been the sun reflected in their lenses that had originally caught Andrew's eye.

"Hello. New glasses?"

"What? Yes, fairly new."

Andrew picked them up and examined them.

"They look like good ones."

"They're quite good. Useful anyway. I've been watching a pair of peregrines."

"Yes, there's a pair that has a nest on the far side of the tor. Where are they?"

"They were over there a while ago," said Markham, pointing to the northeast. Andrew raised the glasses and looked that way but couldn't see them. He lowered the glasses and suddenly realized that the way Markham had been lying, he couldn't have been looking to the northeast. If he had been looking anywhere, it had been to the northwest. He raised the glasses again, looking in that direction, and found himself looking down at a house with a high stone wall around it that was just off the road that led to Bath.

"I always forget about that house there," he said. "It's

down in that combe and you can't really see it from the Downs, just from up here."

"I know," said Markham.

"Look," said Andrew, lowering the glasses. "We'd better talk."

"About what?"

"About why I'm here." Putting down the glasses, Andrew sat down cross-legged next to Markham and told him about the headmaster's summons and what he had had to say to him.

"I had a feeling that old Slyke had his eye on me," said Markham.

"It's clear he has," said Andrew. "Do you feel like telling me what you've been up to?"

Markham turned and looked at him. He was quite fair, had a very open face, and blue eyes. It was only when you looked at them closely that you realized they had shadowy, troubled depths.

"You told the headmaster you weren't going to tell him what I told you—if I did tell you anything—no matter what it was."

"That's right."

"I don't have to ask you whether I can trust you. I know I can." He looked off toward the school. "It's strange. There's something I've got to decide. And I felt from the beginning that if I could talk to one person about it, it would be you."

"Why?"

"I don't know. I suppose partly because I know I *can* trust you and partly because of some of the things you've done. I mean . . . well, your stepfather is an inspector with Scotland Yard, isn't he?"

"Yes, he is. But what do you mean by things I've done?"

"I know you never talk about it, but I've heard that you've been involved in several of his cases. That you had been, as a matter of fact, even before he and your mother got married."

"It's true I've known him for some time. And my mother has too, but. . . ."

"I said I know you don't like to talk about it, and you don't have to. The truth is, I'd like to tell you what's been happening, and I'd like to hear what you've got to say about it."

"Go ahead."

"It began a little over a week ago. I was on my way across the Downs to the old Roman camp. You know where that is."

"Yes."

"I was just going past the tor here when I met this woman."

"What kind of woman?"

"I don't know how to describe her. I mean, I don't know how *you* would, but . . . she was about average height, dark hair and dark eyes, and very pretty."

"How old?"

"I don't know. I'm no judge of women's ages, but she looked about the same age as the mothers of the youngest first-formers at school."

"Middle to late twenties, then. Was she from around here?"

"Oh, no. She was from London."

"How do you know?"

"She said so later on. But even if she hadn't, I'd have known it from the way she was dressed—in something light gray and gauzy and ruffly—and the way she talked. She was very much a lady."

"Was she alone?"

"Yes and no. She was alone near the tor, but she had come in a carriage and the coachman was waiting with the horses on the road about two or three hundred yards away."

"All right. Go on. I gather you talked to her."

"Yes. She seemed surprised to see me there, asked me if I lived nearby. I told her about the school and she seemed surprised at that, too—said she hadn't known it was there. Then I said good-bye and left."

"That's all you said to one another?"

"That's all we said then. I went on toward the old camp and I kept thinking about her, wondering who she was and what she was doing there. I had a feeling that she was worried and upset about something, and I wondered what it was. Finally I turned around and went back, thinking I'd see if she was still there."

"Was she?"

"Yes. And she seemed very glad to see me again. She said she'd been thinking of going after me because she was in desperate straits and I looked as if I could be trusted, and she wanted to know if she could tell me about it."

"And of course you said yes."

"Yes, I did. Do you think I shouldn't have?"

"I don't know. Let's hear what those desperate straits were."

"First of all, she said she wasn't going to tell me her real name because it would be better if I didn't know it, but I could call her Mrs. Grey."

"Lady Jane Grey?" said Andrew with a smile.

"You mean the one who was queen for nine days? I don't think so. I think it was because of the color of her dress. Anyway, that was when she told me she was from London and what the difficulty was."

"And what was it?"

"She had been married for several years to a man she had met at the house of a friend. He was quite a bit older than she was, but very wealthy, and for the first few weeks the marriage went well, then it became somewhat stormy."

"Stormy how?"

"It turned out her husband drank a good deal, had a violent temper, and carried on with other women. The friend at whose house she had met him admitted that she had been worried about the marriage but had decided not to say anything to her. Then, a little over three years ago, she had a child—a boy she named Michael—whom she loved very much. So much that from then on she didn't care what her husband did because she had her son and that was all that mattered to her. Then, a few months ago, things suddenly took a turn for the worse."

"In what way?"

"Something happened to her husband mentally. She wasn't sure whether he had always been slightly mad and no one had really been aware of it or whether this was something new, but he suddenly began accusing her of being interested in other men and claimed she was planning to leave him."

"And this wasn't true?"

"Oh, no. Absolutely not. She said her only real interest was her boy. Well, her husband knew that, and the next thing she knew he had taken the boy when she was out visiting a sick friend, hidden him somewhere, and refused to tell her where."

"That, I suppose, was to keep her from leaving him."

"Exactly. He said that he knew that as long as he had the boy she wouldn't leave and that, in any case, she was making a sissy of him and it was time someone else had a hand in bringing him up."

"What did she do about it?"

"She went to see a solicitor who told her that although what her husband had done was beastly, it wasn't illegal.

That since he was the boy's father, he had a perfect right to keep the boy wherever he wanted. When she asked what would happen if she brought suit against her husband to force him to let her have custody of the child, he said she would lose."

"It sounds quite stupid and very unfair, but I think I've heard of cases like that. What did she do?"

"She hired a private detective to try to find out where the boy was hidden."

"And did he find him?"

"Yes. It took some time and cost her quite a good deal of money, but the detective finally found that the husband was keeping the boy in that house over there, the one in the combe."

"I thought it might be something like that. Then what? What did she want you to do?"

"How do you know she wanted me to do something?"

"It's logical to think that she would. She wouldn't have told you her problem for no reason."

"No, I suppose not. And she did ask me to do something for her. She was fairly sure the boy was in the house there—the detective had said he was. But she wanted to know who else was there, taking care of him. So she asked me if I'd watch the house, let her know."

"So that's what you've been up to."

"Yes."

"Was it she who gave you the field glasses?"

"Yes."

"Why does she want to know who else is in the house?" Markham sat up, looked away, then looked at Andrew.

"She didn't say, but I think she's planning to steal the child back again."

"That would be my guess. How do you feel about it?"

"I don't know." He paused. "Yes, I do. I think it's terrible that she shouldn't be allowed to have her own child! Her husband doesn't really care about the boy. He only took him to hurt her, so . . . well, I've not only been watching the house at all different hours but, if she'd like me to, I'll help her get the child back again."

"Yes," said Andrew. "That was something else I rather expected."

"Well, what do you think about it? I know some people would say it was wrong, but why is it any more wrong for a wife to take a child away from a husband than for a husband to take him away from his wife, the child's mother?"

Andrew sighed. He knew it was more complicated than Markham realized or would be willing to admit. For with his mother dead, it would be strange if he *didn't* want to play the brave knight, didn't want to help a damsel in distress.

"I know how you feel," he said. "But before I tell you what I think, I'd like to meet your Mrs. Grey."

"Well, you can," said Markham. "And very soon, too."

"What do you mean?"

"She's coming back today at about four-thirty."

"That *is* soon. All right. I'll wait."

"Good," said Markham, pleased. He picked up the field glasses, looked through them at the house down in the shallow valley, and said, "Would you like to see the boy?"

"Yes," said Andrew.

Markham gave him the glasses, and he looked through them at the boy who had just come out of the house accompanied by a gray-haired woman who must have been his nurse. Andrew only had a chance to catch a glimpse of him, see that he was a good-looking, golden-haired child and that he did not look at all happy, when the two of them moved toward the rear of the garden and were hidden by the brick wall that enclosed it.

He continued to look at the house, particularly at the gate that led into the garden. If it wasn't locked—and it seemed to have only a latch—that would be the best way in to get the boy. Someone would have to create a diversion, of course, get the nurse and anyone else who might be there away from the garden. But if that were done, then seizing the boy should be fairly easy.

"May I have the glasses?" said Markham.

Raising them, he looked toward the road beyond the house.

"I think. . . ." he said. "Yes, here she comes."

Andrew turned. A brougham had come over the crest of the hill and was moving toward them.

"Where are you supposed to meet her?"

"Near those oaks," said Markham, nodding toward a grove of scrub oaks that grew just off the road. "We'd better go down there."

Hanging the glasses around his neck, he led the way down off the tor and across the rolling terrain of the Downs, over the tough, wiry grass, past patches of heather and broad expanses of wild flowers: buttercups and Queen Anne's lace, bird's-eye, hawkweed, and wandering sailor.

"What will you tell her about me?" asked Andrew.

"I'll tell her that you're a friend of mine," said Markham. "Can I say that?" he asked with a touch of shyness.

"Of course. She's going to assume then that you've told me what she's planning to do."

"And of course I have."

Yes, you have, thought Andrew. But that doesn't mean I approve of it.

They trotted on, past a bank of golden broom. Then, coming around the stand of oaks, they saw the carriage. It had drawn up just off the dusty road, the coachman standing at the horses' heads. He was a small man with a narrow face and dark eyes. He was wearing a squarish bowler and a brown whipcord jacket with matching breeches tucked into Newmarket boots. He looked less like a coachman than a groom, but that may have been what he was.

At first Andrew did not see the woman who called herself Mrs. Grey, but then she stepped out from under the trees and he saw that she was very much as Markham had described her: a large straw hat and a gray dress with a wide sash and ruffles at her throat, not very tall but quite pretty. Her eyes widened when she saw Andrew.

"Hello," she said to Markham. "I was afraid something had happened when I found you weren't here."

"We were up on the tor," he said. "We waited there till we saw you come over the hill. This is my friend Tillett."

"How do you do?" she said, giving him her hand. "I take it you know why I'm here."

"Yes. Markham told me."

"I won't ask if I can trust you. If you're his friend, I know I can." Her hand was soft, her eyes dark and warm. "What have you found out?" she asked Markham.

"Well, besides the woman you told me about—either your husband's woman friend or someone he's engaged to be in charge of the place—there's a nanny who does nothing but take care of the boy. There's also a cook and a gardener. They both sleep there, and I think they're husband and wife."

"I think so, too," said Mrs. Grey. "At least, that's what I was told. But I've found out something much more important than that. Tomorrow morning the woman will be going away, into London, and she will be gone all day. So tomorrow will be the ideal day to do what I'm planning to do."

"How do you know that?" asked Andrew. "That she won't be there?"

"I'd rather not tell you. I think the less you know, the better."

He nodded. It was of course true that if they were ever questioned about what was going on, it would be better if they could say they didn't know.

"Do you know when and how you're going to do it?" asked Markham.

"I know how. The when will depend on the two of you."

"On us?" said Andrew.

"Yes. On when you can get away from school—so I suppose it will be about this same time. As to how, that depends on the two of you also—on how much you'll be willing to help me."

"We'll do anything!" said Markham impulsively. "Anything at all! At least—" He broke off. "What do you think, Tillett?"

"I don't know," said Andrew.

It was all happening much more quickly than he had thought and not at all in the way he had expected it would. He had been very smug in thinking he understood how and why Markham had become involved, and now here he was wanting to be a part of it too. Why? Because Mrs. Grey was pretty? Because it would make him feel manly to be able to help her? Perhaps. But, at the same time, if his mother were in similar difficulties, what would he think of anyone she asked to help her who wouldn't?

"I don't know," said Andrew again. "I'd like to know just how you're planning to do it."

Mrs. Grey had been looking at him, studying him.

"I'll tell you," she said simply, quietly.

Andrew was silent after she had finished. He walked over to the road and looked up to where he knew the house was hidden in the shallow valley. He studied the Downs between there and where they stood, noting that it was mostly downhill. Then he came back to where Markham and Mrs. Grey were waiting, watching him.

"It certainly sounds as if it should work," he said. "All right. I'll do it. We'll do it."

3

The Knights Errant

"What time is it?" asked Markham.

"Twenty minutes after four," said Andrew.

"They should be here soon, then."

"If they're on time, yes."

"I think they will be. They were very prompt yesterday."

"They?"

"Well, she—Mrs. Grey. Do you think we'll ever find out what her real name is?"

"We may."

"How?"

"If it all comes off and there's something about it in the newspapers."

"I never thought of that. I suspect there are lots of things I never thought of." They were lying out on the tor again, the glasses between them. Andrew picked them up and looked toward the slate-roofed house in the combe.

"Is the boy still in the garden?" asked Markham.

"Yes," said Andrew, trying to see exactly where he was. He could see the nanny, but not the boy. However, she was saying something to someone, so he must be there.

"Hello," said Markham. "Who's that?"

"Where?"

Markham pointed to some figures that had come over the ridge that ran across the Downs just north of the valley. It took Andrew a moment to adjust the focus of the glasses, and by that time the figures had stopped moving.

"They look like Gypsies," said Markham.

"They are," said Andrew.

There were two of them: one tall and dark with long mustachios, gold rings in his ears, and a red bandanna tied around his head, and the other shorter and wearing a high-crowned, wide-brimmed hat. They had been walking next to a brightly painted caravan, drawn by a dappled Clydesdale.

"I wonder what they're doing," said Markham.

"Looks as if they're getting ready to set up camp," said Andrew. For now the shorter of the Gypsies was unhitching the horse, while the taller, mustached one had strolled around to the rear of the caravan and was taking a black iron pot from a hook near the rear wheels. "Here," he said, handing the glasses to Markham.

"Yes, they do seem to be setting up camp," said Markham. "Do you think there'll be more of them?"

"Hard to say. I don't see any others, so they're probably alone. Poor chaps. They may be in for a rather rough time."

"Why do you say that?"

"Don't people always suspect Gypsies of kidnapping children?"

"Oh. Yes." He swung the glasses toward the road. "There they are." Even without the glasses, Andrew could see that the brougham had come over the crest of the hill and stopped there. Markham glanced at the long, striped muffler they had tied to a bush next to them. "Do you think they've seen our signal?"

"We'll know in a minute." Then, as the brougham's driver took out a handkerchief and blew his nose, "Yes, they have."

The agreement had been that when they arrived at the tor they would tie a scarf or muffler to the bush to show that they were in place and that, when the driver saw it, he would take out his handkerchief and use it to indicate that he had.

"All right," said Andrew, jumping to his feet, pulling off the muffler, and tying it around his throat. "That's it. We'll have to move fast now."

He slid down the steep top part of the tor, then began running over the springy turf of the Downs toward the house. He paused when he came to the edge of the shallow combe in which the house was set and glanced around. Markham was close behind him, holding the glasses, so that they would not swing wildly as he ran.

"All right?" asked Andrew.

Looking a little worried, Markham nodded. Moving more carefully and quietly now, they worked their way down the side of the combe to the rear of the house. There they stopped again, hiding behind a hawthorn about ten feet from the gate that led into the walled garden. Andrew would have liked to crawl up to the gate and see if it was open, but he knew that was dangerous. He would wait, as they had agreed, for the diversion. If it was locked, he was sure that with a leg up from Markham, he could climb over it.

Crouching there behind the hawthorn, they heard the carriage come in from the road and stop at the front door of the house. The knocker rattled, then the front door opened. They could hear voices, but not what was being said. The driver was supposedly asking directions. Then Mrs. Grey was to get out and join in the conversation and either say she felt faint or fall as if she had fainted.

There was an exclamation from the front of the house, voices were raised, then a woman—probably the cook who had opened the door—called, "Mrs. Woolsey! Mrs. Woolsey, come quickly! The poor woman's fainted!"

A door closer at hand—the door that led from the garden into the house—opened and closed suddenly and vigorously.

"Now!" said Andrew, jumping to his feet. He ran to the garden door and tried the latch. It lifted, and he opened the door. "You stand cavey," he said quietly and urgently to Markham. "I'll get the boy."

Nodding, Markham brushed past the rosebushes that edged the garden, hurried to the door that led into the house, and stood there listening to what was going on at the front door. Andrew, meanwhile, had gone the other way to where the little boy was standing, holding a stuffed woolly lamb.

"Hello," said Andrew. "You're Michael, aren't you?"

Staring at him with eyes that were wide with attention but with no surprise, the boy nodded.

"I'm Andrew. Your mother sent me. Would you like me to take you to her?"

His face lighting up, the boy nodded again, more enthusiastically this time.

"Good. Here we go, then." Swinging the boy, still clutching the lamb, onto his back, he called to Markham. "We're off. Get the garden door," and he ran out through the door and along the combe to the point where the sides were the least steep and it was the easiest to climb back up to the Downs. Behind him he heard Markham close the door that led into the garden, then he was running alongside him.

"Well done," he said. "Need any help?"

"No," said Andrew. "We're fine."

The boy, arms around Andrew's neck and feet locked

around his waist, was laughing with delight at the sudden and exciting ride. He cried out with dismay when he dropped his woolly lamb, but became quiet when Markham picked it up and showed it to him.

"I'll carry it for you," he said, and the boy nodded.

They were up on the Downs now, and though they had some distance to go, it was, as Andrew had noted before, all downhill. Twice Markham offered to take the boy, and both times Andrew shook his head. He did not want to take the time to make the change, and he did not know how the boy would react to it—he was still quiet and seemed happy.

On they ran, over the springy turf, circling around so that they reached the road on the far side of the trees. By that time Andrew was panting a little and had a stitch in his side.

"Mummy?" said the boy as Andrew disengaged his arms from around his neck and set him down.

"She'll be here soon," said Andrew.

"I think I hear the carriage," said Markham, giving the boy his woolly lamb.

A moment later the brougham drew up, the door opened, and Mrs. Grey jumped out, followed by an older, rather severe-looking woman in a nurse's uniform. Without a word, Mrs. Grey picked up the boy and handed him to the nurse, who—also without a word —got back into the carriage. Then she turned to the boys.

"You were wonderful!" she said to them. "I'll never forget you. Never!"

She threw her arms around Andrew and kissed him on both cheeks. He was very conscious of the softness of her lips and of something else. The scent she had on? It may have been. In any case, there was something familiar about the embrace, something he could not identify.

She kissed Markham as she had Andrew, then followed the nurse into the carriage. The door slammed, the sharp-faced coachman with the square bowler hat cracked his whip, and the brougham went rattling off down the chalky road in a cloud of white dust.

Andrew and Markham stood there staring after it, and Andrew, for one, had some curiously mixed feelings. He was moved by the woman's kisses and what she had said. At the same time, there was something a little odd about her behavior, something he could not quite put his finger on.

"Well, that's that," he said. "You were very good all through that. In fact, top-hole."

"Thank you," said Markham, pleased.

He *had* been good, doing everything that needed to be done with the speed and precision of the other half of a pair of good Rugby backs. And it was only then that Andrew realized how skillfully the whole thing had been planned. As far as he knew, no one had seen him or

Markham, and there was no one who could connect them with Mrs. Grey. At the same time, no matter what anyone might suspect, who could blame Mrs. Grey for the kidnapping when she had been with the people in the house the whole time until she drove away?

4

Disaster!

Andrew was not sure when he first began to feel uneasy about their exploit. He and Markham had to hurry to get back to school in time for tea call-over. Then there was prep and he had a great deal of reading to do for English and didn't have a chance to think about anything else.

The next morning, though, when he started going back over what had happened, he realized that one of the things that had been bothering him was Mrs. Grey's behavior toward the boy. If she loved him as much as she claimed and hadn't seen him for as long as she said, how was it that she hadn't made more of a fuss over him, hugged him and kissed him before she handed him over to the nurse? On the other hand, she was clearly anxious to get away—as she should have been—and she may have decided to hold off on the emotional part of her reunion with the boy until she was sure they were really out of danger.

He had something much more important to worry about, however, and that was what he was going to say to the headmaster. For while he could now assure him and Mr. Slyke that there was no longer any reason to be concerned about Markham, he could not tell them why.

As a result of all this, he was fairly sober when he left the house on his way to chapel. Chadwick, who was his best friend at school, walked with him, chattering about a New Zealander who would be playing for Oxford in that year's varsity match and who was supposed to be as great a batsman as the incomparable W.G.

The absolute knowledge that something was wrong came to Andrew as they approached the chapel and saw the crowd in front of it. For some reason the boys were going in much more slowly than usual—in fact, only one or two at a time.

"Hello!" said Chadwick. "Here's a go. What's up?"

"I don't know," said Andrew.

"Why, there's old Bartram and a copper," said Chadwick, seeing the headmaster standing at the chapel door with a constable. "Who's the other cove?"

As soon as Andrew saw the other man—a sharp-eyed, middle-aged man in pepper-and-salt tweeds—he knew that he was a police officer, too, and a very senior one. But remaining discreet, he said, "I don't know."

They were now close enough so that they could see

precisely what was happening. As each boy reached the open chapel door, he was halted and his gray school blazer was examined quickly but carefully by either the constable or the plainclothes police officer, who stood one on each side of the door. Then he was waved on into the chapel. Though the headmaster took no part in the actual search, it was clear from the expression on his face and the way he looked at each boy as he approached the door, that he was very much involved in the proceedings.

"Well, if that doesn't beat Banagher!" said Chadwick, who had a weakness for colorful slang. "What are they looking for, blood?"

Before Andrew could answer, there was a sudden flurry of excitement at the door. With an exclamation, the constable reached out, picked up the arm of the boy who had just come abreast of him and said something to the man in the tweed suit. He examined the boy's sleeve, too, and called the headmaster's attention to it. The headmaster glanced at it, at the boy's face, and his face became grim. He said something to the boy and the two men, and the three of them turned and started to come down the steps through the crowd of waiting boys. When Andrew saw the boy's face, his worst fears were confirmed. For of course it was Markham. His face pale, Markham looked at Andrew and then away, walking past him without saying anything to him.

"Isn't that Markham?" said Chadwick.

"Yes."

"What have they nobbled him for?"

"All right, boys," said the headmaster, who had remained at the open chapel door. "That will be all. In you go now." And with nothing to hold them up, the boys began to pour past him into the chapel.

"Coming?" asked Chadwick, starting up the chapel steps.

"No," said Andrew. And turning, he began walking quickly the other way, following Markham, the policeman, and the man in the tweed suit, who were crossing the quadrangle on their way to the headmaster's quarters. He caught up with them just as Markham and the man in the tweed suit went in, but as he tried to follow them, the policeman stopped him.

"Just a second, young fellow, me lad," he said. "Where do you think you're going?"

"In there."

"Is that so?"

"Yes. I've got to go in!"

"Oh, hello, Tillett," said the headmaster, coming up behind him. "I thought it was you."

"Yes, sir. Something's happened to Markham, hasn't it?"

"Yes, something very serious indeed."

"I gathered that. And while I don't know what it is, if anything's wrong I'm just as much to blame as Markham. In fact, I'm probably more to blame."

"Why do you say that?"

33

"Because you asked me to keep an eye on him, didn't you?"

"Yes, I did." His face still grave and troubled, he looked thoughtfully at Andrew. "All right. Perhaps you should come in."

Nodding to the policeman, he led Andrew through the entrance hall and into his study. Besides Markham, who was standing there pale and rigid, and the man in the tweed suit, who was leaning casually against the desk, there was a woman in the room, a woman Andrew had never seen before. She was probably in her middle twenties, quite fair and very attractive. She sat on a chair in a corner of the room wearing a checked cotton dress and a dark straw summer hat. And though she wasn't weeping now, she clearly had been, for her face was drawn, her eyes red, and she held a damp handkerchief in her hands.

"Before we go any further," said the headmaster, "I think some introductions are in order. This is Mrs. George Vickery." The troubled woman inclined her head in acknowledgment. "This," he said, indicating the man in tweeds, "is Detective Inspector Gillian of the Somerset Police. And these two young men, students of this school, are Christopher Markham and Andrew Tillett." Andrew and Markham both bowed. "I now turn the proceedings over to you, Detective Inspector."

"Thank you, sir," said Gillian. "I'd like to begin by asking Markham where he was yesterday afternoon at about four-thirty."

"I was out on the Downs," said Markham.

"Where on the Downs?"

"On the top of the tor—Bodmin's Tor."

"Did you stay there—on the tor?"

"No, sir. I didn't."

"May I ask why you want to know this, Detective Inspector?" asked Andrew.

Gillian looked at him with an exaggerated show of patience.

"You're probably not familiar with police inquiries, Master Tillett—there's no reason why you should be— but the fact is that I have a good reason for asking the questions that I am asking."

"I'm sure you have," said Andrew. "But I'd like to know what that reason is."

"Now look here, Tillett," said Gillian, his patience starting to slip.

"Please don't, Detective Inspector!" said Mrs. Vickery suddenly and emotionally. "Don't get angry and formal and official. These are good boys. I can tell that just by looking at them. And I'm sure they'll help us if they can. It's my son," she said, turning to Andrew. "My boy, Michael. He was taken away, kidnapped, yesterday afternoon at about four-thirty. If you know anything about it—anything that will help get him back—please, please tell us!"

Andrew felt as if he had been kicked in the pit of the stomach. For as soon as she said it, he knew that what

Mrs. Vickery had said was the truth. The boy they had helped steal was *her* son—not the son of the woman who had called herself Mrs. Grey. He glanced at Markham and saw that he, too, realized that they had been duped and had done a terrible thing. For though he had been pale, anxious and worried before, now he looked really ill, as if he might even faint.

More to give himself time to think than for any other reason, Andrew asked another question.

"What made you think that Markham—anyone here at school—knew anything about it?"

Apparently quick and intelligent enough to recognize that he could now count on the boys' support and did not need to trap them, Gillian held up a small gilt button.

"We found this outside the garden after Mrs. Vickery came and told us the boy was missing. It had a lion rampant on it, which I knew was the school emblem, and I suspected that it might be a button off a school blazer. I came to see Dr. Bartram about it last night. He confirmed my suspicions, and though he did not know how or why any boy here could be involved in what had happened, he suggested that we examine the boys as they came to chapel this morning."

"I see," said Andrew. He glanced at Markham, who was looking at the left sleeve of his blazer where there was now only one button instead of two. "Sir," he said

36

to the headmaster, "before we go any further into this—and of course we'll tell you everything we know, do everything we can to get the boy back—may I have your permission to send a telegram?"

"To whom?"

"My stepfather."

"Ah. Yes. That might be a very good idea."

"Does this have anything to do with what we're talking about?" asked Gillian.

"If I read young Tillett correctly, it does," said the headmaster. "His stepfather is Inspector Wyatt of the London Metropolitan Police."

"I see," said Gillian. "I would not be at all averse to some help from Scotland Yard in this. I'll be glad to send any telegram you write, Tillett. And at the same time I'll send one of my own, asking officially for any assistance the Yard can give us."

"Thank you, sir," said Andrew. "But in the meantime, while you're waiting for an answer to your telegram, may I suggest that you start making inquiries about a black brougham hired from a livery stable somewhere in this area—probably in Bath—that was drawn by a bay mare and a bay gelding, the mare with a white blaze on her face and the gelding with a blaze on his chest."

"Oh?" said Gillian, looking at him sharply. "Yes, I can do that. Do you have any idea who can have hired it?"

"I don't know his name, but I can describe him. He

was short, dark, narrow-faced, and wiry. He was wearing a brown, squarish bowler, whipcord jacket, and breeches tucked into Newmarket boots. He might be either a groom or an ex-jockey, but he's some kind of professional who knows and can handle horses."

5

Enter the Inspector

Andrew's stepfather arrived a little before noon the next day. He had answered Andrew's telegram with one of his own announcing the time of his arrival. As a result, all those interested were waiting in the headmaster's study: Mrs. Vickery, Inspector Gillian, Andrew, and Markham, as well as the headmaster himself.

Andrew was a little surprised and more than a little disconcerted when the carriage drew up and, after his stepfather got out, he turned and helped Andrew's mother out.

As they came up the walk and the headmaster and Andrew went to the door to greet them, Andrew realized that he should have known she would come. After all, he had not been specific as to what was wrong, merely said that it was something serious and requested his stepfather's help. And, that being so, his mother would naturally think it concerned something that involved the school and was therefore more her responsibility than her new husband's.

The headmaster, who had met her when Andrew first came to the school, greeted her warmly, and she introduced him to Wyatt. Then she turned to Andrew, looking searchingly into his eyes before she kissed him. Wyatt did the same when they shook hands. Then they went into the study where the headmaster introduced them to the others.

Wyatt raised an eyebrow when he was introduced to Inspector Gillian, responded modestly when Gillian said he had heard a good deal about him, and then they all sat down.

The headmaster began by thanking Wyatt for coming so promptly and suggested that perhaps Inspector Gillian might be the best person to explain the problem.

Gilliam nodded and, as simply and succinctly as possible, told of being summoned to Mrs. Vickery's house, of being told that her son was missing, and joining in a hunt for him on the chance that he might have wandered away by himself. It was only after they had found no trace of him that they began searching the garden and found the button that led them, the next morning, to Markham.

"I assume," said Wyatt, looking at Markham, "that you can tell us how the button from your blazer was found outside the garden."

Markham nodded miserably, but at this point Andrew said, "Excuse me, sir, but I think I might be the best one to tell this part of it."

"Go ahead," said Wyatt, who had clearly been waiting to hear what Andrew's connection with all this had been.

And so Andrew told them what had happened from his point of view, beginning with the headmaster's concern about Markham and ending with the moment when they gave the boy to Mrs. Grey and she drove off with him.

There was silence for several minutes when he finished. Though he had been sick with guilt ever since he had learned the truth, dreading his mother's and stepfather's reaction, he knew now that there was no reason to be concerned about that at least. There was nothing but sympathy and understanding in his mother's eyes and gravity in his stepfather's.

"Well, I can see why you said the matter was serious and urgent," said Wyatt.

"Don't be too hard on the boy," said the headmaster. "I feel I'm very much to blame in the matter. If I hadn't spoken to him about Markham, he never would have become involved."

"I don't think we need be hard on anyone," said Wyatt. "I don't think anyone regrets what has happened more than Andrew and Markham. In any case, we're not here to fix the blame for this tragic event, but to try to do something about it. So I would like to ask Mrs. Vickery a few questions."

"Of course," said Mrs. Vickery. "I'll be glad to tell you anything you want to know."

"How long have you been living in your present house?"

"A little less than a year."

"And before that?"

"We lived in Cambridge."

"Your husband was at the university?"

"He had been. We met there while he was still an undergraduate, married when he finished his studies and took his tripos, and stayed on afterward because he was continuing his studies in some areas and doing some writing. Then, as I said, a little less than a year ago, when our son was about two years old, we moved here."

"Why was that?"

"George, my husband, thought it would be healthier for Michael. Cambridge, as you know, is very damp. And it did seem to be better for him. We were very, very happy here—even more so than we'd been at Cambridge—and then—" Suddenly her voice broke and she began weeping. "Forgive me," she said, sobbing. "I've been trying to be brave, but it's all been too much for me. First there was the sudden, frightening word that something had happened to George—I still don't know exactly what, where he is—and then this. . . ."

At the first sign of distress, Andrew's mother, Verna,

went over, knelt down next to her and put her arms around her—not saying anything, just holding her.

As they waited in silence for her to recover, there was a knock on the door. The headmaster went to it, opened it, and had a whispered conversation with one of the masters. Then, excusing himself, he went out. By that time Mrs. Vickery had stopped weeping and said, "I'm sorry. I'm all right now. Let's go on."

Wyatt glanced at Verna, who nodded, moved her chair over, and sat down next to Mrs. Vickery.

"I'd like to know a little more about your husband," he said. "He's a writer?"

"I wouldn't say that. He does some writing on economics and history, but not a great deal."

"What does he do then? It's difficult to put this without seeming to pry, but . . . where do you get the money to live on?"

"He has a private income. Not large, but sufficient for us to manage."

"Do you know the source of that income?"

"Yes. A family company, based somewhere on the Continent—I think in Paris—that does importing and exporting. His parents are both dead, so he gets the major part of the income."

"Does he have anything to do with the company?"

"Yes. Not a great deal, but something. He goes over once or twice a year to see how things are going. He's over there now. At least, he was when—" She broke off again.

"You got word that something had happened to him."

"Yes."

"Can you tell me exactly what that word was—where it came from?"

"It was a telegram from Bucharest in Rumania. It said George had had a serious accident and was feared lost; it was signed Vadja."

"Who is Vadja?"

"The man in charge of the family business. At least, that's what George has always said."

"Did you get in touch with this Vadja, ask him for details?"

"No. I don't know exactly where the company is based, so I don't know where to reach him. But I went to London—to the Rumanian Embassy—to see what they knew—and they said they didn't know anything about it."

"About either your husband or this Vadja?"

"That's right. But they said they'd inquire. Then, the day before yesterday, I got a telegram from a solicitor in London named Jessup saying he had word for me about my husband. I went hurrying in, found Mr. Jessup in Gray's Inn, but he didn't know what I was talking about, said he hadn't sent the telegram, didn't know my husband or anything about him. When I got home, I found that my boy was gone."

"Sounds like a trick to get you away so the boy *could* be taken," said Wyatt, looking at Inspector Gillian.

"That's what I thought," said Gillian. "But it would have to be someone who knew that her husband was missing."

"Yes," said Wyatt. "Now has there been any word from the kidnappers? Any demand for ransom?"

"No," said Mrs. Vickery. "Not a word."

"Have you any idea why the boy was taken? If it's for money, you don't seem to be a particularly good choice. I mean, unless you're mistaken about your husband's finances, you're not rich."

"We aren't," said Mrs. Vickery. "We're comfortable, but certainly not rich. On the other hand, I'll give anything I have to get my boy back!"

"Of course," said Wyatt. "We'll wait and see if we hear from the kidnappers. And when I get back to London, I'll look into your husband's disappearance. But in the meantime, I'd like to see if I can develop any leads here—which means going over the boys' testimony again."

"Excuse me, Inspector," said Gillian. "There are also the Gypsies."

"You mean the ones the boys saw setting up camp when they were on top of the tor."

"That's right."

"Have you talked to them?"

"No. One of my constables did right after the boy was

45

reported gone. He asked them if they'd seen anything, and they said they hadn't. But I thought it was rather strange that they should have appeared up here at the very moment the boy was stolen. So I sent the same constable up there to bring them to the local police station. They should be there now."

"You haven't charged them?"

"No. I just said there were a few questions I'd like to ask."

"There are a few I'd like to ask also. Perhaps we can talk to them together. But first, as I said, I'd like to go over what the boys told us again." He had taken out a notebook when he first began talking to Mrs. Vickery and had made several notes in it. Now he turned to Markham. "You saw this woman who called herself Mrs. Grey three times. Andrew saw her twice, and the last time doesn't really count. Could you give us as accurate a description of her as you can?"

"Yes, sir," said Markham. "I'm not good at ladies' ages, but Tillett thought she was in her middle or late twenties—medium height—quite pretty, with dark brown eyes, and wearing this rather ruffly light gray dress."

"Complexion? Color of hair?"

"She was very pale—that was one of the reasons I believed her when she told me how upset she was, what desperate straits she was in. As for her hair, it was black."

"Forget the black hair," said Verna abruptly and unexpectedly. "It was probably a wig."

"Why do you say that?" asked Wyatt with a good deal of interest.

"It's just a feeling I have," said Verna. "May I ask a few questions?"

"By all means, my dear."

"Did she really say she was in desperate straits?" Verna asked Markham. "I mean, did she use those exact words?"

"Yes, she did."

"Now tell me about the dress she was wearing. You said it was gray—light gray—with ruffles?"

"Yes, the ruffles were around her throat. And it had a wide sash."

"What sort of material was it made of?"

"I don't know. I'm afraid I don't know anything about that sort of thing. Something very soft and a little crinkly."

"Andrew?"

"I may be a little better at it than Markham, but not much. Georgette?"

"That's possible."

"Excuse me," said Wyatt. "But is the fabric important?"

"It may be," said Verna, undisturbed. "Especially when it's combined with some other things. Now she wore that dress when you saw her for the first time—when she told you about the desperate straits that she was in."

"Yes," said Markham.

"And she wore it the second and third times you saw her also."

"Yes."

"I think I see what you're getting at," said Wyatt thoughtfully.

"Well, please don't say anything about it and don't interrupt," said Verna. "Andrew, would you say it was an appropriate dress to wear up here in the country?"

"I hadn't thought about it before, but . . . no. No, it wasn't really appropriate at all."

"Yet she wore it— not just the first time Markham saw her, but the two times you saw her also."

"Yes."

Verna thought a moment. "You're very observant, Andrew, and you have a good memory. You stood close to her at least twice, didn't you?"

"Yes. When I first met her, I shook hands with her, and just before she got into the carriage and went off with the boy, she kissed me."

"Yes. Now close your eyes and think back to that moment—the moment she kissed you. Do you remember it?"

"Yes."

"Was there anything about it that seemed familiar— that reminded you of anything?"

"Yes. It's interesting that you brought it up. I had a feeling about it at the time, wasn't sure what it was, but . . . it was a smell!"

"The scent she had on?"

"No, it wasn't a scent. It was something else—something that was familiar, but that I couldn't place."

"Well, keep your eyes closed and be patient. She has just kissed you and you smell something familiar. Perhaps you can't place it, identify it, but does it remind you of anything?"

Eyes closed, he tried to recapture the moment. "Yes." It was ridiculous, but he said it anyway. "It reminds me of you."

"How?"

"I'm not sure. Not of you yourself, but of something connected with you. Some place you've been? Some place where I've visited you?" Then it came to him. "Your dressing room at the theater!"

"In other words, the smell was the smell of greasepaint."

"Yes! Yes, exactly!"

"Oh, well done, darling!" said Wyatt. "Well done indeed!"

"In other words," said Inspector Gillian, "you think that the woman who said she was Mrs. Grey was an actress."

"Yes," said Verna. "I thought so from the beginning— from the time Markham said that she told him she was in desperate straits. People just don't talk that way outside of bad plays and bad books. And of course it would make sense to get an actress to play the distraught mother—

then you could be sure of getting a convincing performance. And of course if she was an actress, you would expect her to wear a costume—a dress that was right for the part she was playing—young, innocent, helpless and bereft—rather than one that was suitable for the place she was going. And finally, of course, besides a wig, she would be made up to look pale and distraught—hence the heavy makeup."

"Yes, I can see all that. And I think it's wonderful that you've been able to determine that she was an actress," said Mrs. Vickery. "But does that really help us very much?"

"It narrows the field down somewhat," said Wyatt. "And it gives us a place to begin."

"Perhaps we can do even better than we have so far," said Verna. "I'd like both of you to think about that woman, Mrs. Grey, again," she said turning to Andrew and Markham. "You've described her general appearance, what she was wearing. Can you tell us anything a little more specific about her that might help us to identify her? A scar? A birthmark?"

"No," said Andrew slowly. "I don't remember anything."

"What about jewelry? Was she wearing any jewelry?"

"I think . . . ," said Markham. "Yes, she was! She was wearing a fairly large pin. A brooch. As I recall, it was pink."

"You're right!" said Andrew. "It was a heart carved out of coral!"

"What about earrings?"

"Yes," said Andrew. "She wore coral earrings, too!"

"And a coral bracelet," said Verna. "A wide one, strings of coral fastened together."

"Yes!" said Markham with excitement. "That's right. She did!"

"That's that, then," said Verna with a sigh of satisfaction. "It was Coral Lumden," she said, turning to Wyatt.

"You know her?"

"Slightly. She's tried out for some of Harrison's productions. I believe her real name is Carol, but when an admirer gave her that coral set, she began wearing it all the time and changed her name to Coral. She thought it would make it easier for managers and directors to remember her."

"Do you know where we can find her?"

"No, but there'll be no trouble about that. If Larry Harrison doesn't know, he can find out."

"Well, I must say I'm bowled over, inspector," said Gillian. "When I heard you were coming up here, I was prepared to be impressed by the way you went about a case. But I never expected to be even more impressed by what your wife did."

"I know. She's a constant revelation even to me."

"You're off to London, then?"

"Yes." Wyatt turned to Mrs. Vickery. "You'll come with us, won't you?"

"If you think that's where my boy is, yes, of course."

"You'll stay with us," said Verna. "We've plenty of room."

"You'd better come with us too, Andrew," said Wyatt. "I'll speak to your headmaster and get permission. You should be there to identify Coral Lumden when we talk to her."

"And may I come too, sir?" said Markham. "Please? After all, what's happened is more my fault than anyone else's, and if there's anything I can do to help find the boy and get him back—anything at all. . . ."

Wyatt exchanged a quick glance with Verna and Andrew, then nodded. "All right, Markham. There's plenty of room for you too. I'll ask Dr. Bartram for permission to take you with us as well as Andrew."

6

The Gypsies

"Put your bags down there," said Inspector Gillian, leading the way into the police station. He had driven them there in his dogcart while Verna went to the house in the combe to keep Mrs. Vickery company while she packed.

Andrew and Markham dropped their bags near the door and joined Gillian and Wyatt at the desk.

"You brought the Gypsies in?" Gillian asked.

"Yes, sir," said the sergeant. "They're in the charge room. But before you go in, there's something here you ought to see." He handed the inspector a report.

Gillian read it quickly, glanced at Andrew, and handed the report to Wyatt.

"You'll be interested in this, too," he said. "When I first spoke to young Tillett yesterday, he suggested that we inquire at livery stables in the neighborhood, particularly in the Bath area, to see if we could find out who had hired a brougham drawn by a pair of horses that he described. Well, the constable I put on it found the livery stable near the railroad station in Bath."

"Who had hired it?" asked Andrew.

"The man you saw driving it," said Gillian. "The man in the Newmarket boots who looked like a groom. But that's not all. While he was there, the constable made some inquiries at the railroad station. And the same man, another man, and a nurse carrying a small boy all took the 6:04 train to London."

"What about the woman in the gray dress?"

"No one mentioned seeing her."

"That's interesting," said Wyatt. "She was probably trying to separate herself from the others. Good for you for making that suggestion, Andrew. And good marks for your constable, too," he said to Gillian. "That confirms what we suspected—that they took the boy to London."

"Right. Do you still want to talk to the Gypsies?"

"Perhaps we'd better. It's probably just a coincidence that they appeared near the house at about the time the boy was taken, but it might be best to make sure."

"I agree," said Gillian.

He opened the door of the charge room and went in. Wyatt went with him and, since no one said anything to the contrary, Andrew and Markham followed.

There were two desks in the room and several straight

chairs. The shorter of the two Gypsies was sitting in one of the chairs, but the taller one, who had apparently been pacing the floor impatiently, stood near the far wall looking at them hostilely. He was even more impressive in person than he had been when Andrew had seen him through the field glasses. He was tall, broad-shouldered, and sunburned and wore a white shirt, open at the throat, and dark trousers tucked into the tops of short boots. Someone else dressed as he was, with gold rings in his ears, a red bandanna around his head, and long mustachios, would have looked theatrical, but he did not. He looked completely natural.

"Good afternoon," said Gillian. "I'm Detective Inspector Gillian of the Somerset Police. And this is Inspector Wyatt of the London Metropolitan Police."

"Well, well," said the tall Gypsy. "Scotland Yard. We're honored."

He had a deep voice, and though there was a faint touch of mockery in it, there was no trace of an accent. Wyatt bowed politely to him, and he bowed in return.

"We'd like to ask you some questions," said Gillian.

"Before you begin," said the Gypsy, "I'd like to know if we're charged with anything."

"No," said Gillian. "As I said, we'd just like to ask you some questions."

"All right. Ask them. If we're not charged with anything, maybe we'll answer, and maybe we won't."

"First of all, I'd like to know your name."

55

"Jasper Lee."

"That's not a very Gypsy name."

"But it is," said Wyatt. "The two most common Romany surnames in England are Lee and Herne."

"Is that true?" Gillian asked Jasper.

"Your friend from Scotland Yard said so. Don't you believe him?"

"Yes. All right. And what's your friend's name?"

"Daniel," said the shorter Gypsy. He did have an accent, quite a decided one. "Daniel Lee."

"Are the two of you related?"

"All the Romanies in England are related," said Jasper. "Even the Lees with the Hernes."

"What do you do?"

"I'm a gry-coper."

"What's that?"

"A horse trader," said Wyatt.

"Yes," said Jasper, looking at him with increased interest. "You *rokra* Romany?"

"No," said Wyatt. "I don't speak it. I just know a few words of it."

"What are you doing around here?" asked Gillian. "They don't raise horses in these parts."

"There's no place in England where they don't raise horses. And anyone who has a horse is willing to at least talk about trading him. But you're right. We're on our way to Exmoor to buy ponies."

"What do you do with them?"

"Drive them to Bristol where we put them on a ship and sell them to the Rumanian Zingari. They're a good market for Exmoor ponies."

"Is that where you came from?" asked Wyatt. "Bristol?"

"Yes. You've asked me quite a few questions. Can I ask you one?"

"Yes."

"Have you found the boy yet?"

"What boy?"

"The one who was stolen yesterday afternoon."

"How do you know about that?" asked Gillian sharply.

"My mother was a *chovihani*, a witch." His companion said something to him, speaking firmly in what may have been Romany, but certainly wasn't English. Jasper nodded. "My *chal* here doesn't like the way I answered that. And he's right. We know about the boy because one of your constables came around last night and asked if we'd seen him. We said we hadn't; and even though he didn't have the proper papers—a warrant—we let him search the *vardo*, our caravan."

"No," said Gillian. "We haven't found him yet."

"Do you have any idea where he might be?"

"Perhaps."

"Where?"

"Before we answer that, can I ask you another question?" said Wyatt. "Why are you so angry?"

"Why?" said Jasper, his eyes flashing. "You're an intelligent man. You even know some Romany. Well, if you're as intelligent as you seem, you shouldn't have to ask that. If you're a Romany, you're an Ishmael, an outcast. And if anything happens, whether its poaching, pilfering, petty thievery, or breaking and entering, you're the first one to be suspected. Isn't that true?"

"Not necessarily," said Wyatt mildly.

"Of course it is! And it's particularly true about something like this! Because aren't Gypsies suspected of child stealing more often than anyone else? When you were a boy weren't you told that if you weren't careful the Gypsies would steal you?"

Again his companion said something to him, and after a moment Jasper nodded. "Again my friend doesn't like the way I've been talking to you. And again he is right. I apologize. Now will you tell us who you think may have taken the boy and where they have taken him?"

"We don't know who took him or why," said Wyatt. "But we think he was taken to London."

"Ah, yes. The Big Smoke. That could well be. Do you have any more questions, Inspector?"

"No," said Gillian. "I think you can understand why we wanted to talk to you. You came here just before the boy was taken, set up camp almost within sight of his house. We thought you might have seen something that would help us find him."

"We didn't. We saw nothing. Since we're Gypsies, you don't have to believe us, but it's true. Anything else?"

"Not right now. What are your plans?"

"Gypsies don't like to make plans."

"Well, if you should make any and they include leaving this area, will you let me know? In other words, we'd like to know where you are in case we want to talk to you again."

"Of course, Inspector. We'll keep in touch with the police."

And bowing to Gillian, to Wyatt and the two boys, to whom he had not said a word, he and the second Gypsy left.

"A strange fellow," said Gillian.

"Very," said Wyatt.

"I have a feeling he was telling the truth about the boy. I don't think he did see anything, and I don't think he did have anything to do with the kidnapping. At the same time, I think he knows a good deal more about the whole affair than he was willing to tell us."

"I agree with you. In fact, if I were a betting man, I'd put a few bob down on it. Though how we're ever going to find out if it's true is more than I can say."

7

Coral

They took an early afternoon train from Bath and were in London a little before six. Wyatt went directly to the Yard to deal with anything that needed his immediate attention, and Verna and Andrew took Mrs. Vickery and Markham home to the house in St. John's Wood. Mrs. Vickery was given one of the guest rooms, and though Markham could have had one too, Andrew thought he might be more comfortable sharing his own room.

Matson had just brought up their bags when, with the most perfunctory of knocks, the door opened and Sara came in. Andrew had tried to tell Markham about her on the way down, but he hadn't found it easy. Could he say she was a friend? She was, of course, and a very good friend. But she was a great deal more than that, just as her mother was a good deal more than the Tilletts' housekeeper. Because a few years before, when Andrew was all alone in London, Mrs. Wiggins had taken him in and acted almost as a foster mother—something Andrew and his mother had never forgotten. But that, of course, was only part of what there was to say about Sara. There were her personal qualities: her enthusiasm, directness, and intelligence among other things. But Andrew had a feeling that Markham would find out about them himself—and very soon.

"I suppose I should have waited till you'd washed and changed," said Sara. "But I couldn't wait any longer."

"I know," said Andrew. "This is Markham. And this is Sara Wiggins."

"Hello," said Sara. "I gather you're at school with Andrew."

"Yes, I am."

"Then, continuing with my deductive reasoning—which is the envy of Scotland Yard—I would guess that whatever happened, you're in on it, too."

"Yes, I certainly am."

"Well, then," she said, turning back to Andrew, "are you going to tell me about it?"

"I don't know."

"Oh." She looked at Andrew more closely, at Markham, and then back to Andrew. "I'm sorry. I didn't realize it was that serious."

"It is, Sara. About as serious as it could be."

"Then I apologize. I never thought it was exactly a joke. I mean, I knew you must have had a very good reason for sending that wire. But it never occurred to me that it might be something you wouldn't want to talk about."

"The trouble is, it's not just me. As you gathered, Markham's in on it, too, and I don't know how he feels about it."

"And of course he doesn't know anything about me, who I am, whether I can be trusted, or anything like that."

"As a matter of fact, I do," said Markham, looking at her with undisguised interest. "Tillett told me a good deal about you. And besides, there's been a certain amount of talk at school about a friend of his—a girl—who's been involved in several cases with him and his stepfather. So, if you want to tell her about it," he said to Andrew, "it's all right with me."

Which is just what Andrew did. When he had finished, Sara, who was usually very quick and impulsive, was silent for a long moment.

"Yes," she said finally. "I can see why you didn't feel like talking about it. Poor Mrs. Vickery."

"We were idiots," said Markham. "I especially. If we don't get the boy back—and soon—I'll never forgive myself."

"Why are you especially an idiot?" said Andrew. "I'm a year older than you, and I've had a lot more experience with things of this sort."

"Stop arguing about who was most to blame," said Sara. "From what you've told me, anyone would have been taken in. What's the next step?"

"Mother's going to try to find out where this Coral Lumden lives, and we're going to go see her, see if she's really Mrs. Grey. And if she is, see if we can get anything from her that will help us find the boy."

"When are you going to do that?"

"Probably tomorrow."

"Then you may know something by the time I come home from school."

"We may."

"I'm not going to say don't worry—I don't see how you can help it—but I am going to say something that you particularly must know, Andrew. And that is that if there's anyone in the world who can get the boy back safe and sound, it's Wyatt."

It took very little time to locate Coral Lumden. Most theater managers keep the names and addresses of aspiring actors and actresses on file, and Verna's manager and friend, Lawrence Harrison, was able to give it to her at once. And so, a little before eleven the next morning, Fred, the Tillett coachman, drove Verna, Wyatt, and the two boys to the address they'd been given in Holborn, just off Shaftesbury Avenue.

Mrs. Vickery had wanted to come with them, but Wyatt had said that he didn't think it was a good idea;

that she might find it difficult to remain calm if she met the woman who had actually taken her son. And somewhat reluctantly, Mrs. Vickery had agreed.

When the carriage drew up, they all studied the house, a rather drab brownstone that looked as if it might be a boarding house. Then Verna got out. They had agreed to let her talk to Coral alone before they appeared.

"What are you going to say to her?" asked Wyatt.

"I don't know," said Verna. "I'll decide when I see her."

And looking very smart in a light shantung suit and a hat with a matching veil, she went up the steps and rang the bell. A maid in a cap and apron opened the door, Verna said something to her, the maid let her in, and the door closed.

"I'm getting out now, too," said Wyatt to the boys. "But I think you should wait here in the carriage for the time being. I don't want her to see you if she should happen to look out the window. When Verna signals for me to come in, you can follow. But hang back a bit."

He got out of the carriage and began to walk casually up and down. After a few minutes the front door opened again and Verna appeared, beckoning to him. He went up the steps and, getting out of the carriage, Andrew and Markham followed him, arriving at the door just before it closed. They went in quickly and quietly. There was a small and rather cluttered sitting room to the right of the entrance hall. Standing in the middle of it and smiling a polite but puzzled smile, was a young woman in a dressing gown that was not too clean. The most striking thing about her was her hair, which was chestnut verging on auburn. It took Andrew several seconds to recognize the woman who had called herself Mrs. Grey.

"And this," Verna was saying, "is my husband, Inspector Wyatt of the Metropolitan Police."

The woman's smile faded. "The police?"

"Yes." By now Andrew and Markham had reached the entrance to the room too. "And I believe you know these two young men."

Looking at them, the woman lost her color completely, went white.

"No wonder you wouldn't tell me what you wanted to talk to me about!" she said to Verna.

"You know them?" said Wyatt.

"Yes. How did you find me?"

"We have our methods," said Wyatt. "In this case, I had a good deal of help from my wife."

The woman, Coral, looked at Verna, then at Andrew. "Tillett," she said. "The other boy said that his name was Tillett, but I never thought. . . . He's your son?"

"Yes," said Verna.

"What do you want?"

"First of all, I think you should sit down," said Wyatt. Coral hesitated a moment, then sat down slowly on the edge of a rather decrepit chair. "Next, I'd like to make sure you understand what a serious position you're in."

"Why do you say that?"

"Because there are very few crimes on our books that are more serious than kidnapping."

"Kidnapping?" She shrank back, looking as if she were going to faint. "But I didn't . . . Merciful Heavens!"

"You know what I'm talking about, don't you?"

"I don't know. If you mean what happened up there in Somerset, I thought it was all straight and aboveboard, just as I told the boys—except that I wasn't the child's mother. But by the time it was over . . . you mean it wasn't true?"

"I don't know what you were told, what you believed, but the boy you helped steal from that house was living with his mother—his real mother—at the time."

"Heaven help me! I should have known there was something wrong! I think maybe I did!"

"Very wrong indeed. Now will you help us get the boy back?"

"Yes," said Coral promptly. "As I said, by the time we got to the end, I had started to feel funny about it. How can I help you?"

"You can begin by telling us how you became involved, who approached you, when, and where."

"All right. It began a little over two weeks ago at an audition for *Cardew's Castle*. That's a new play that Millerton is casting," she said to Verna, who nodded. "The part I was trying out for was the second lead—the young sister—and I thought I was pretty good, but the director didn't and said, 'Thank you very much. Next please,' so I left. But as I went out, a man who had been sitting in the back of the theater followed me out. He said he thought I'd been very good, and, while he wasn't in the theater, he had a job for me and was I interested? I said I was as long as it wasn't white slavery, so we went into a pub just up the street and he bought me a gin and It."

"Was this the man who got you to steal the boy?"

"Yes."

"Tell me about him—his name, what he looked like, who he said he was."

"Well, he said his name was Benson and he was a private detective. He was in his middle thirties, not much taller than I am, but he looked taller because he held himself very straight. Kind of like a soldier, know what I mean?"

"Yes."

"He had a little beard and dressed kind of sporting— a checked suit and a soft hat—but all very nice."

"He said he was a private detective?"

"Yes, and that he needed help in a case he was handling for a client."

"What kind of help?"

"The story that he told me was the same as the one I told the boys—that this woman's husband had taken her child out of spite and she wanted to get the child back.

The only difference was that he said she was so upset she was in a nursing home and he wanted me to act as the mother to help get the child back."

"And you believed him?"

"I don't know. Why not?"

"Why did he need someone to pretend to be the mother? Why didn't he just get someone to take the child?"

"I don't know that either. I suppose he thought it would be simpler to have someone tell the story I told and get someone else to take the child."

"Simpler and safer. And safest of all if he could get someone to help you who wouldn't ask any questions. Someone like a young, romantic, trusting boy."

"Yes," she said faintly.

"Did he know about young Markham?"

"Yes, he did. He'd been up there before, looking around. He went up there with me the first time, told me about this boy he'd seen. He said he wasn't sure he'd be there and I'd be able to talk to him, but that if I could it might be very useful. Then when the boy was there and when I got him to agree, first to watch the place and later to help me, he was very pleased."

"Did he tell you how to dress, how to act, and all the rest?" asked Verna.

"No. He said he'd leave that to me. I liked that, creating the character myself. I decided to wear a wig because my hair is too easy to remember. And of course I put on makeup to look worried and upset."

"How much did he pay you?" asked Wyatt.

"Fifty quid." She looked at him unhappily. "I needed the money. Needed it bad."

"Yes," said Wyatt. "All right. Markham and Tillett got the boy, turned him over to you. The man who called himself Benson was in the brougham with you at the time?"

"Yes. He and a woman—a kind of nurse. They had come up to Bath from London together. When we had the boy, we drove back to Bath, and they dropped me at the hotel where I had changed my clothes and made up. Benson paid me the money he'd promised me and told me to stay there overnight, not to come back to London with them."

"Did you?"

"No, I was suddenly nervous, anxious. I changed my clothes and took the next train back to London—the one that they were on, as it happened."

"Did they see you?"

"No. I saw them, waited till the last minute, and then got into a Second Class carriage at the back of the train."

"Did either Benson or the nurse give the boy anything when you handed him over?"

She looked down unhappily. "Yes. The nurse gave him something she said was a sweet, and almost immediately after that he fell asleep."

Wyatt nodded. "They would have had to do that, give him something to make him sleep so he wouldn't create a disturbance. All right. You arrived back in London. Then what?"

"I hung back again, waited till they had left before I left myself."

"When you say 'they,' who do you mean?"

"Benson, the nurse, and the man who hired the brougham in Bath and drove it."

"How did they leave Paddington?"

"The coachman hurried out and got a cab—a four-wheeler—and they all got in it."

"You didn't by any chance hear where they were going?"

"No."

"You've been honest and have been trying to be helpful, and I appreciate it. Now is there anything you can tell us about any of them that might help us to find them and the boy?"

She thought a moment. "Just this. I don't think Benson was English. I'm quite sure the nurse wasn't."

"Why do you say that?"

"Well, it wasn't that Benson had an accent, he didn't. It was . . . well, as if English weren't really his language. Know what I mean?"

"Yes."

"As for the nurse, after she gave the boy the sweet and he fell asleep, she said something to Benson in a language that wasn't English."

"You don't know what it was?"

"No."

"What about the coachman?"

"Oh, he was English, there's no doubt about that. In fact, Cockney."

Wyatt, who had been making notes all the time Coral was talking, looked up at her.

"As I said, you've been helpful—as helpful as you could be—and I won't forget it. Now do you have any family or a friend outside of London you could stay with for a while?"

"Well, I have an aunt who has a boardinghouse in Bournemouth. Why?"

"I'd just feel better if you went away for a while."

"You mean I might be in danger here?"

"You might be. I think we're dealing with some quite professional and probably dangerous people. And if they should find out that you've talked to the police, they might be very angry about it."

"Oh. All right. I'll go stay with my aunt. I'll leave this afternoon."

"I'll send a constable around to take you to the station," said Wyatt, standing up. "Give him your address in Bournemouth, and as soon as I think it's safe for you to come back, I'll send you a telegram."

"And when you do come back," said Verna, "come and see me. I might be able to help you find something in the theater."

"Oh, thank you," said Coral, her eyes getting misty. "I feel awful about what happened. If there's anything more I can do to help, I'll do it. And I hope you get the boy back safely and very soon."

"So do I," said Wyatt soberly.

They were all quiet as they left the boardinghouse.

"I'm glad she tried to help us," said Markham. "It not only made me like her better, it made me feel a little better about myself—not like quite such a fool."

"I know what you mean," said Andrew. "Though she didn't tell us very much we didn't know, did she?" he asked Wyatt.

"No. She merely confirmed several things we suspected. But then it would have been too much to expect her to tell us the really important things."

"Like who that man Benson really is," said Verna. "Why they took the boy, and where they've got him."

"Exactly."

"How do you find that out?" asked Markham.

"The way we always do. It's wonderful when you suddenly get an idea and solve a case with a flash of brilliance. But most of the time you solve it with plain, solid, patient police work. And that's what we're going to have to do here."

Fred had opened the carriage door, and Wyatt helped Verna in. "Good-bye, my dear," he said. "Thank you for your help. I'll see you tonight."

"You're very welcome," she said. "Not that I was all that helpful. And good luck!"

8

The Coachman

Andrew and Markham were in the garden when Sara came home from school—Markham sitting on a bench and Andrew pacing impatiently up and down.

"Where have you been?" Andrew asked, frowning.

"You know where. At school."

"Well, you're home late."

"I am not. If anything, I'm early. I slipped out a few minutes before music was over. But what's the rush?"

"I don't know," said Markham. "He's been like this ever since we got home."

"Oh?" said Sara. She looked at Andrew. "What happened with Coral Lumden? Did you find her, talk to her?"

"Tell her," said Andrew, and Markham did, recounting everything that had happened during their visit to the Holborn boardinghouse.

"But that's good," said Sara. "Isn't it?"

"I suppose so," said Andrew. "That part anyway."

"What do you mean by that part? Did you think she was going to tell you everything you wanted to know? Or are you upset because it's out of your hands now? Because Peter and Scotland Yard have taken over and there's nothing more you can do."

"Of course not," said Andrew, a little uncomfortably because there was some truth in what she said. "I am a little disappointed that she couldn't tell us more than she did. But there's something else. I'm worried about Mrs. Vickery."

"Why? Where is she?"

"We don't know," said Markham. "We wanted to tell *her* what had happened when we got home, but Matson said she'd gone out—he didn't know where."

"Does your mother know?" Sara asked Andrew.

"I don't think so. She didn't come home with us. We dropped her off at Harrison's office."

"Well, what if Mrs. Vickery did go out?" Sara said. "There's nothing wrong with that, is there?"

"It depends on where she went."

"I thought you didn't know where."

"I don't, but I've got some ideas about it."

"Well, if you're worried and upset," Sara said, looking at him thoughtfully, "she's even more worried and more upset—not just about her boy, but about her husband, too."

"Go on," said Andrew encouragingly.

"There's nothing more she can do about finding the boy—not at the moment—and anyway that's what the police are trying to do. But there might be something she can do about finding her husband."

"What's that?" asked Markham who had been following the exchange with interest.

"Well, there are several odd things in this whole matter of her husband. But one of the oddest is that a grown man has disappeared and no one knows anything about it."

"In other words, you think she went to the Rumanian embassy again," said Markham.

"It's what I'd do if he were my husband," said Sara.

"Is that what you think too?" Markham asked Andrew.

"Yes."

"But why should that worry you?"

"If the people there were lying—and I'm sure they were—how do you think they'll feel if she presses them, accuses them of lying?"

"Oh," said Markham, getting up. "What are we waiting for?"

"We *were* waiting for Sara."

"Well, I'm here now," said Sara, dropping her bag of school books on the bench. "Do you know where the embassy is?"

"No," said Andrew as they started up the street toward

Wellington Road. "I thought we'd stop off at the post office and look it up in the directory."

Since Mrs. Vickery had been there before, she knew where the embassy was—on Court Street, near Eccleston, in Belgravia—but that was not of much help to her. The footman who let her in turned her over to the very imposing person in knee breeches and a velvet coat who wore a large seal on a silver chain around his neck, the embassy majordomo, or steward. She remembered him from her last visit, and he apparently remembered her, for he bowed to her very politely.

"Good afternoon, madam," he said.

"Good afternoon. I am Mrs. George Vickery." She gave him her card. "I would like to see the ambassador."

"I am sorry, Mrs. Vickery. When you were last here I told you that the ambassador was ill and could see no one. I am afraid he is no better and so is still unavailable."

"Oh. Whom did I see then?"

"Colonel Katarov, the first secretary."

"That's right. I was too upset to remember his name. Could I see him?"

"I am afraid he is not here at the moment. If you will tell me where you can be reached, the colonel will get in touch with you and make an appointment to see you as soon as he can."

Mrs. Vickery shook her head stubbornly. "I'm sorry. I must see him today. I'll wait."

"But, madam. . . ."

"I said I must see him! May I wait?"

"He may not return for some time, but . . . of course, madam. Will you come this way?"

He led her to a small anteroom, seated her in a straight-backed chair, bowed, and left her. An hour went by. There was a good deal of coming and going; she heard the front door open and close several times, but apparently the first secretary had not returned for the steward did not come to get her.

The three young people stood in front of the Court Street Hotel, a small hotel next to a pub, and looked at the four-story marble-and-limestone building across the street. A wrought-iron fence surrounded the areaway; there was a bronze plaque with a seal on it next to the door and a flag over it.

"Is that it?" asked Markham.

"It must be," said Andrew. "The number's right."

"Of course it is," said Sara. "The question is, who goes in?"

"Couldn't we all go in?" asked Markham.

"I suppose we could," said Andrew. "But it would seem a little odd, as if we were a delegation."

"I don't see anything wrong with that," said Sara. "In a way, we *are* a delegation, and—" She broke off as Andrew stiffened. A brougham with yellow wheels and a crest on the door had come up the street and stopped in front of the embassy door. Putting his hand in his pocket, Andrew pulled out some coins and apparently, in his haste, dropped several.

"Help me pick them up, Markham," he said urgently, turning his back to the street and bending down. "Sara, move over and stand in front of us."

Markham glanced at Andrew, at the carriage, then going pale, he bent over also and began helping to pick up the coins. Sara, moving over so that she was standing between them and the carriage, turned and watched as the coachman, a thin-faced man in a uniform and a top hat with a cockade on the side, jumped down off the box and opened the carriage door.

"Is it the coachman?" she asked under her breath.

"Yes," said Andrew, still bending down. "He's the one that drove the coach that the Vickery boy was taken away in. What's he doing?"

"The man who just got out is talking to him. Now the coachman is touching his hat and getting back onto the box. His passenger's going into the embassy. The embassy people must know him because they're bowing. Now the coachman's shaking the reins, and the carriage is going up the street."

"Do you think he has anything to do with the embassy?" asked Markham. He and Andrew had both stood up as the carriage moved off and were watching as it approached Eccleston Street.

"It's possible," said Andrew as it turned the corner.

"There's one way to find out. Sara. . . ." He didn't have to finish the sentence.

"I'm off," she said, hurrying down the street in the opposite direction from the coach. She turned left at the corner, walked to the mews that ran behind the row of houses, and stood there, looking up the narrow, cobbled alley. Sure enough, the carriage came into the mews from the other end, drove up some forty or fifty feet, then turned into a stable. She waited until the coachman had closed the stable doors, then walked through the mews, counting the stables. The coachman had gone into the fourth one from Eccleston Street. She went back to Court Street by way of Eccleston, counting the houses. The embassy was the fourth building.

"He went into the embassy stable," she announced to Andrew and Markham, who were waiting where she had left them.

"Oh, well done!" said Markham. "That means he has something to do with the embassy. He's probably their coachman."

"Yes," said Andrew.

"What do we do now?"

"See if Mrs. Vickery's there. And if she is, go to the Yard and report," said Andrew.

"I'll go," said Sara. Then, as Andrew hesitated, "Don't be dim. It's got to be me in case the coachman is around somewhere. After all, he knows the two of you."

"That's true," said Andrew. "All right, go ahead. But

if you're not out in five minutes, we're coming in after you."

Sara walked across to the embassy and used the knocker. A footman in knee breeches and a clawhammer coat opened the door and looked at her with some surprise.

"Good afternoon," said Sara. "I'm looking for Mrs. Vickery. Is she here?"

The footman looked at an older man with closely cropped white hair who wore a seal on a silver chain around his neck.

"Mrs. Vickery?" he said with a slight accent. "Yes, she is. Come this way."

He led her to a small anteroom where Mrs. Vickery, her eyes dark and her brow furrowed, sat stiffly in a straight-backed chair.

"Why, Sara," she said. "What are you doing here?"

"Looking for you."

"How did you know where I was?"

"Guessed it. Andrew and Christopher Markham are outside. We'd like you to come with us."

"I can't, Sara. I'm waiting to see the first secretary. I've got to see him to find out whether he has any word about my husband."

"I know. But it's important that you come with us." She jerked her head slightly, indicating that she couldn't talk in front of the white-haired steward, who stood behind her, waiting.

In spite of her distress, Mrs. Vickery understood.

"I see. In that case, of course I'll come." She rose. "Will you tell the first secretary that I was here and that I will be coming back again, probably tomorrow?" she said to the steward.

"I will, madam," he said, bowing.

It was shortly before this that Wyatt got the first results from his police work. There was a knock on the door of his Scotland Yard office, and Tucker, the large and deceptively quiet sergeant who had worked with him since he became an inspector, opened it, spoke to whoever was out in the corridor, and came back in.

"It's Rickett," he said.

"Oh, yes." Rickett was a young constable who had just been assigned to the Detective Division. Wyatt glanced at the schedule on his desk. "He was covering Paddington, wasn't he?"

"Yes, sir. With Walker and Flynn."

"Send him in."

"He's got two men with him, sir."

Wyatt sat up even straighter.

"Then by all means send him in."

Tucker opened the door again, and Rickett came in, followed by two men who wore battered billycock hats and could not have been more obviously cabdrivers unless they had carried whips. One was short and red-haired and looked like a wise old fox. The other was tall and as lugubrious-looking as a bloodhound.

"Sir!" said Rickett, saluting.

"Hello, Rickett," said Wyatt. "What's the good word?"

"Well, it's not quite as good as I'd like it to be, sir. But it's something. I don't know if you remember what my assignment was."

"To cover Paddington, see if you could find anyone who had seen the three people we were interested in."

"Right, sir. I've got two men who did."

"Two?"

"Yes, sir. I suggest you start with Burke here." He indicated the shorter, red-haired man.

"Full name?" asked Tucker, who had seated himself and opened his notebook.

"Nappy Burke. Christened Napoleon, but Nappy's what they calls me. Now I understands you're interested in Zack Macy, guv'ner," he said to Wyatt. "Is that right?"

"I don't know," said Wyatt. "Who's Zack Macy?"

"Well, that's what the orficer told me. Said you wanted information about a party—a woman carrying a child and two men—who came off the Bristol and Bath train at a little after seven two days ago."

"We do," said Wyatt. "You saw them?"

"Why else would I be here?"

"To make sure there's no mistake, would you describe them?"

"The woman was a nanny. At least, she was wearing a nanny's duds. She was carrying the child."

"How old?"

"Oh, I'd say three or four years old. A boy. He was asleep."

"And the others?"

"One of them was a toff—little beard, checked suit, and a soft hat. The other was Zack."

"Would you describe him, too?"

"Still not sure, eh? Right, he's kind of mean and ratty looking—narrow face and dark eyes. And he was dressed like he usually is when he's not working—brown bowler, cord jacket and breeches, and Newmarket boots."

"Yes," said Wyatt, letting his breath out with a sigh. "What can you tell us about him?"

"Old Zack? I can tell you plenty. Used to be a jockey, steeplechase as well as flat racing. Used to be pretty good, too, till he got barred from the tracks."

"Why was he barred?"

"Lots of reasons—riding off, interfering with other horses, roughing up other jockeys. But mostly for throwing races."

"Ah? Then what?"

"Became a cabby for a while. That's when I knew him. Then he got sent up for robbery and assault and lost his cabman's license. He dropped out of sight for a while, and the next I heard he was swanking around and saying he had a cushy job as a coachman."

"Do you know where?"

"No, I don't."

"All right. They got off the Bristol train—Zack, the

other man, and the nurse carrying the child—then what?"

"I was first on the cab rank. They came out with Zack leading. He takes one look at me, walks by me, and takes the next cab in the line, the one behind me."

"In other words, he knew you, knew you knew him, and didn't want you to know where he was going."

"That's what I'd suss."

"All right. They got into the next cab. Who was driving it?"

"Moseby, sir," said Rickett, indicating the other cab-driver. "That's why I brought him."

"Full name?" asked Tucker.

"What? Oh, 'Orace. But mostly they just calls me Mose."

"Right," said Wyatt. "Do you remember the party that Burke, here, has been talking about?"

"Well, yus. I didn't at first. But then, when Burke reminded me about it, I did."

"And do you remember where you took them?"

"I do. Sackville Hotel on Sackville Street."

"You're sure about that?"

"Sure as herring's fish—because there was something very rum about it."

"What was that?"

"I pulls up in front of the hotel. They gets out. The toff pays me, gives me a tanner tip. Then, 'stead of going into the hotel, they gets into another cab and goes off again."

Wyatt whistled softly. "It sounds as if they wanted to make absolutely sure no one knew where they were going."

"Of course," said Nappy Burke. "He's a wido cove, that Zack Macy."

"He seems to be. Well, thank you both for coming in. If either of you see Macy again—or if you even get a clue as to where we can find them—let us know."

The cabmen assured him that they would do that and left.

"I'm sorry, sir," said Rickett, who had remained behind. "I know you hoped for more than we got, but I thought I'd better bring them in and let you talk to them just the same."

"Of course. It wasn't your fault that we ended up out of the money. And I guess it was too much to expect that we'd pick up the trail this quickly."

"Yes, sir," said Rickett. He opened the door, started to go out, and hesitated. "There are some people out here, sir. I think they want you."

"See who they are, will you, Tucker?"

Tucker went to the door.

"It's our two young friends, a friend of theirs, and a lady, sir."

"Oh? Well, have them come in. This is a bit of a surprise," Wyatt said as he introduced Tucker to Mrs. Vickery and Markham. "Though I shouldn't be surprised at anything you two do," he said to Andrew and Sara.

"I hope you don't mind, sir," said Andrew, "but we

found out something we thought would interest you."

"Well, we're in the market for it—though we did come up with a little something ourselves."

"What was that?" asked Sara.

"We've identified the coachman who drove the carriage that took your son to Bath, Mrs. Vickery. His name is Zachariah Macy. He's an ex-jockey and ex-cabdriver with a criminal record. We traced him to Paddington. Unfortunately we haven't been able to pick up his trail after that."

"Well, we did," said Sara. "That's why we're here."

Wyatt stiffened.

"Let's hear it," he said. He listened intently to their report. "I said I shouldn't be surprised at anything you two came up with, but I must say you seem to have outdone yourselves."

"Hear, hear!" said Tucker.

9

The Embassy

"I was rather busy after you left the Yard yesterday," Wyatt said at breakfast the next morning. "But I was able to make some arrangements I thought necessary, and I'm sure you can guess what our next move will be."

"You're going to the embassy," said Sara.

"I am. I'm meeting Tucker in front of the Court Street Hotel in half an hour. But before I go, I'd like to ask you a few questions, Mrs. Vickery."

"Of course. Anything!"

"We've checked with the Post Office and, unlike the telegram from the London solicitor, which was false, the telegram that you received from Bucharest about your husband was actually sent from there. However, I'd like to know a little more about this man named Vadja who sent it. First of all, what's his last name?"

"I don't know. Whenever my husband mentioned him,

he'd just call him Vadja. I mean, he'd say, 'I just got a letter from Vadja, and I have to meet him in Paris or Berlin or Vienna.' "

"And you're sure he's connected with the family business?"

"Yes, I am."

"What makes you so sure?"

"Well, whenever the matter of money came up—whenever we needed a large sum for something like the house in Somerset—George would say, 'I'll write to Vadja and see what we can do about it.' "

"But it was clear that it was your husband who was in charge and not Vadja."

"Yes, definitely."

"Did it ever occur to you that there might not be a Vadja? That he might be a convenient fiction to allow your husband to go to the Continent and meet someone else?"

"You mean another woman? Of course it occurred to me. At least, I thought about it, wondered about it. But I'm sure—absolutely sure—that it's not true. If a woman's really honest with herself, I think she always knows when a man is being unfaithful to her. And I'm sure that George wasn't. That he loved me and no one but me."

"Very well. I'm sorry, but I had to ask that. One last question. Were those letters from Vadja always routine or did they sometimes disturb your husband?"

"It's interesting that you should ask that. I've been

thinking about it, and . . . well, in the beginning they were more or less routine. George would just shrug and smile when he got one. But lately he did seem to find them more and more disturbing."

"I see. Well, thank you, Mrs. Vickery," he said, getting up. "I'm off now."

Andrew exchanged a quick glance with Markham.

"Can we come too, sir?" he said. "I mean Markham and me. Sara has to go to school."

"Why?" said Wyatt, frowning.

"Well, of course, we'd like to. But the chief reason is that I think we might be useful."

"What makes you say that?"

"I don't know what you plan to do or say when you go into the embassy. And we're not asking to be allowed to go in there with you—that would be ridiculous. But I suspect you're going to ask about Macy. Well, if he gets scared and runs, wouldn't it be a good idea to have someone outside who knows him and can follow him?"

"What do you think the arrangements I talked about consisted of?"

"I was fairly sure that that's what you meant. But the fact is that Markham and I do know him, while anyone else you station around there would only have a description to go on."

"That's true. I don't like the idea of your following him—even trying to follow him—at least, alone. But. . . ." He glanced at Verna and saw that she was willing to leave the decision to him. "All right. I know what we can do about it. Come along."

Wyatt and Tucker walked up Court Street and paused in front of the building.

"Rumania," said Tucker, looking at the bronze plaque next to the door. "Where's that when it's at home?"

"On the Black Sea. One of the Balkans."

"Oh," said Tucker as if that were just another way of saying trouble. "One of those, eh?"

"Yes," said Wyatt, going up the three low steps. "One of those."

He rapped sharply with the polished brass knocker, and the door was opened almost immediately. He nodded to the footman who had opened the door, glanced at the white-haired man who stood in the center of the entrance hall facing him. A steward, he thought. Or perhaps a majordomo, if there still are such things.

"Good morning, sir," said the man, bowing slightly. "How may I help you?" He had a deep, pleasant voice and only a trace of an accent.

"Good morning. I'd like to see the ambassador."

"I regret, but that is impossible. The ambassador, Count Rozarin, is ill."

"I'm sorry to hear that. Who is in charge, then?"

"Colonel Katarov, the first secretary."

"I would like to see him, then."

"Of course." He had been studying Wyatt and it was

clear that if he had not liked what he saw, he would not have said of course. "May I have your name?"

"Inspector Peter Wyatt of the London Metropolitan Police." He held out his warrant card as identification. "And this is Sergeant Tucker."

The majordomo glanced at Tucker, at the card, and returned it.

"If you will wait a moment, sir, I will speak to the colonel."

He crossed the entrance hall, knocked at the door of a room just off it, and went in. Wyatt and Tucker looked around—at the marble floor, the crystal chandelier overhead, and the staircase just ahead of them that curved gracefully as it ascended.

"Quite a place," said Tucker approvingly. "Balkan or not."

Wyatt nodded. The majordomo came out of the room to their left.

"Will you come this way, gentlemen?" he said. "The colonel will see you."

He stood aside to let them in. It was a large room with books on two walls and looked more like a library or a study than an office. There were two men in it. The man sitting behind the desk had white hair, which he wore rather long and brushed straight back. He was a distinguished-looking man and could have been taken for a scholar if his eyes had been less cold and hard.

"Good morning, inspector," he said, getting up and

offering Wyatt his hand. "I am Colonel Katarov and this is Captain Benesh."

Wyatt and Benesh nodded to one another. Benesh was shorter than Katarov, clean-shaven, stocky, and powerful looking with the carriage of a soldier.

"And this is Sergeant Tucker," said Wyatt. The colonel and the captain both nodded coolly. "I was very sorry to hear that the ambassador was not well. Has he been ill for very long?"

"For about two weeks now," said the colonel.

"What's wrong with him?"

"One of the malarial fevers. Like me, he was a military man before he became a diplomat. But I do not think you came here to commiserate with us about his excellency's health. That would be more in the province of your Foreign Office, would it not?"

"It would. I have actually come to see if you could give me some information about an Englishman named George Vickery who seems to have disappeared in Bucharest about ten days ago."

"Vickery," said the first secretary. "It sounds familiar."

"Mrs. Vickery, his wife, came here about five days ago," said Benesh. "She claimed she had received a telegram saying that something had happened to her husband in Bucharest."

"She was here again yesterday," said Wyatt. "But why do you say she claimed she had received a telegram? Didn't she show it to you?"

"As a matter of fact, she did. But we questioned our telegraph people in Bucharest, and they had no record of it, knew nothing about it."

"Well, I queried our people at the Post Office here, and they gave me a copy of the telegram, which they say was unquestionably sent from Bucharest and came by way of Paris. Here is it." And he gave the first secretary the telegram.

"I see. Yes," said the first secretary examining it. Then, looking up, "May I ask why you are so interested in this man, Inspector? Is he of some particular importance?"

"How long have you been here in England, Colonel?" Wyatt asked rather coldly.

"Four years. Why?"

"If you have been here for any time at all, you should know that every Englishman is important to us—whoever he is and no matter where he may be."

"Well, of course, we did look into the matter immediately after Mrs. Vickery was here, but Bucharest said that they knew nothing about such a man."

"Aren't foreigners required to produce their passports when they arrive at a hotel in Rumania?"

"Of course."

"Well, were the hotels of Bucharest queried to see where Vickery was staying?"

"I don't know. We will inquire."

"May I point out that it is over a week now since Mrs.

Vickery was first here? And that, as I said before, she was here again yesterday?"

"Yes, yes. It has all been very unfortunate. But I can assure you that we will now give the matter our earnest attention. In fact, Captain Benesh will give it his *personal* attention."

"Yes, I will," said Benesh.

"Good. Because if there is no definite word about Vickery by tomorrow, I shall take the matter up with our Foreign Office."

"I have assured you that we will do our best," said Katarov stiffly. "Now was there something else?"

"Yes. You have a coachman here named Macy—Zachariah Macy?"

"Yes, we do have a coachman," said Katarov slowly. "Is his name Macy?" he asked Benesh.

"I believe it is," said Benesh.

"Could I talk to him?"

"May I ask why?"

"Yes. I believe he can give me some information that might help me on another case. I'd like to ask him a few questions."

"Well, naturally we—and of course he—will be delighted to help you in any way we can. Will you get this Macy fellow for the inspector, Captain?"

"Of course, Colonel. Immediately." And he left the room.

"You said the ambassador has been ill for about two weeks now?" said Wyatt.

"About that long."

"Has a doctor seen him?"

"Why do you ask?"

I thought if you didn't have a doctor you call on regularly, I might recommend one—someone who is familiar with military and tropical diseases."

"That's very kind of you, but of course we do have our own doctor, someone who has been taking care of all of us for some time now."

"I see."

Wyatt made no attempt at further conversation but merely stood there, looking at Katarov and around the room, and Tucker did the same. Katarov folded his hands and sat there quietly, waiting. Finally the door opened and Benesh came in.

"I'm very sorry, Inspector," he said. "But Macy does not appear to be here."

"I'm sorry to hear that. Do you have any idea when he'll be back?"

"I'm afraid I don't."

"Too bad." He took out a card and a pencil and wrote something on the back of the card. "Will you give him this when he gets back and tell him that I must see him as soon as possible? I'm sure he knows where Scotland Yard is."

"I'm sure he does, too," said Benesh, taking the card. "I'll see that he gets this."

"Good. Thank you very much for the time you've given us, Colonel," he said to Katarov. "I'll be back tomorrow to see what information you have for me about George Vickery."

"What? Oh, yes."

Benesh opened the door for them, and they went out. As they reached the entrance hall, an elderly woman in what looked like a nurse's uniform came out of a door that led to the rear of the embassy. She carried a tray on which there was a bowl of soup and some thin slices of toast.

"The ambassador's lunch?" said Tucker casually.

"What? Yes, I imagine it is," said Benesh.

"Doesn't have much of an appetite, does he?"

"One doesn't when one has been running a fever. Goodbye, Inspector. I'll see you tomorrow."

"Yes, Captain."

The majordomo bowed to Wyatt and Tucker, a footman opened the door, and they went out into Court Street.

"Captain Benesh," said Tucker. "If I was a betting man, I'd give you six quid to a cracked egg that that was Mr. Benson."

"He certainly fit the description we got from Coral Lumden."

"What about Zack Macy? Do you think he was there?"

"It would be interesting to know. And even more interesting to see what happens when he hears we want to talk to him. Who's watching the back of the embassy?"

"Rickett. And of course young Andrew, Markham, and good old Fred."

"I see you've got Leaming here," he said, nodding to a uniformed constable who was leaning against a pillar-box and making no attempt to conceal the fact that he was watching the embassy.

"Yes, sir."

"Good. The Running Footman won't be open yet," he said, nodding to the pub that was just up the street, "but we can have some coffee in the lounge of the hotel."

"Yes, sir," said Tucker. "I told all concerned that we'd be in one place or the other."

They took a window table that allowed them to look out at the street and ordered coffee and scones. Tucker had finished his second cup of coffee and his third scone when Wyatt, who was facing the embassy, said, "Don't turn around, but someone just came out of the embassy and is walking this way. I know him, but I can't place him. See if you can."

"Tell me when he's opposite us."

"Now," said Wyatt a moment later.

Tucker turned slightly and looked at the man who was coming down Court Street—a slight, pale man in a dark suit that didn't fit too well and a rather battered bowler. He was nondescript and looked like a poorly paid clerk.

The only thing about him that was at all unusual was the fact that he walked with a decided limp.

"I know him, too," said Tucker. "He's done something to make himself look different, but . . . of course! It's Stub Pollard!"

"The cat burglar?"

"The king of them until he broke his leg and had to give it up. He's shaved off his mustache, lost some weight, and isn't dressed as flash as he used to be. But it's Pollard all right."

"I wonder where he's going."

"Shall I tell Leaming to follow him?"

"No. He came out of the embassy and I suspect he may go back there. In fact, this may turn out to be very interesting."

It was about fifteen minutes after this that Rickett, walking back and forth in the mews behind the embassy, heard a carriage approaching and stepped into a doorway to let it go past. When it appeared, it turned out to be not a carriage but a growler, or four-wheeled cab. He moved closer to it when it stopped opposite the rear entrance of the embassy. His job was to follow anyone who *left* the embassy, not keep them from entering, but he felt he should look at anyone who was going in.

The man who got out of the four-wheeler was slight and rather ordinary looking, but then if he were anyone of importance he would have gone to the embassy's front entrance. He paid the cabdriver, and as he started into the rear service door, Rickett noticed that he walked with a limp. He also noticed that the man had left the door of the four-wheeler open. He was about to whistle to call this to the cabby's attention when there were running footsteps; a crouching figure ran out of the embassy's rear entrance and jumped into the four-wheeler. The door slammed, the cabdriver cracked his whip, and the cab started out of the mews.

"Hoy there! Wait! Stop!" shouted Rickett, running after it. But the growler didn't stop. In fact, it went even faster as the cabman cracked his whip again. And just as it reached the end of the mews and turned right toward Belgrave Road, the man who had jumped in, looked out of the small back window, grinning.

For the last half hour, the Tillett brougham had been standing outside one of the neat brick houses on Eccleston Street, which crossed Court Street. Fred, the Tillett coachman, was standing next to it with his back to the mews when the four-wheeler drove into it. He didn't turn around, but he didn't have to, for he had carefully stopped the carriage so that he could see the mews reflected in the brougham's side lamp.

Spitting on the cloth in his hand, he bent down and continued polishing the already gleaming door panel.

"Growler in the mews," he said quietly.

"I see it," said Andrew, kneeling next to Markham in the back of the carriage.

"Well, keep your head down," said Fred, who enjoyed this sort of thing as much as he would riding a Derby winner. Then, in the distance a door slammed, a cabby cracked his whip, and the growler came out of the mews toward them. "Well?"

"Yes!" said Andrew as the four-wheeler turned a sharp right past them and he caught a glimpse of the man in the back. "It's Macy! After him!"

Without seeming to hurry, Fred climbed onto the box, untied the reins, and sent the pair of bays trotting smartly after the cab. He kept his distance, even dropped back a little as the four-wheeler bowled down Belgrave Road and only closed in on it a bit as it turned left at Vauxhall Bridge, following the Thames by way of Milbank and the Victoria Embankment.

"Can't he go any faster?" asked Markham, who was now sitting on the edge of the brougham's rear seat, trying to peer out of the window.

"Afraid he'll get away?" asked Andrew.

"A little."

"Well, don't be. There's no better coachman in London than Fred."

"Just in London?" said Fred, guiding the horses around an omnibus and cutting in front of a hansom.

"I didn't want to say the best in England because I know how modest you are. Any idea where he's going?"

"Way east. Maybe as far as Limehouse."

It was a good guess. With the brougham following, the four-wheeler went past the Tower, turned into the world of warehouses and sheds that surrounded St. Katherine's Docks and came out on Wapping High Street just before the river turned south again at Limehouse Beach.

"I think he's stopping," said Fred, pulling up a little and dropping behind a huge brewer's dray.

Again his instincts were correct. The growler drew up in front of The Eight Bells, a riverside pub, and Macy got out.

Paying the cabby and giving him an even larger tip than he'd promised, Macy went into the pub. He knew the landlord, who fenced goods on the side, and a short while later Macy was taking off his coat and stretching out on the bed in the not-too-clean room over the pub.

"All right, me boyos, time!" called the landlord, rapping on the bar with a bung starter.

Protesting from sheer force of habit, Macy pushed his glass away. He'd had more than enough to drink long before closing time, and he knew it. But that hadn't stopped him. That, of course, had always been one of his problems. Whenever he started drinking, he found it very difficult to stop.

He staggered a little as he got to his feet and blinked in surprise as someone took his arm, steadying him and saying, "Easy, me old brown son."

"Oh, it's you, Stub. What are you doing here?"

"Came to see you, Zack," said Pollard. "Make sure you were all right."

"Oh, I'm right as rain, Stub, and even wetter."

"I can see that, Zack. How about a little fresh air? Might make you feel better."

"I wouldn't mind that, Stub. Not at all."

Waving to the landlord, he went out of the pub with Pollard still holding his arm.

"Which way?" he asked when they were standing in the cobbled street.

"How about the river? I always like the river at night."

"The river it is," said Macy, stumbling a little as he led the way down toward the docks. "That was a right slippy bit of work, getting me away like that. Right slippy."

"I'll tell the captain that. He'll be pleased. He's been worried about you."

"Worried?"

"Yes. He didn't like it that them Scotland Yard rozzers has been coming around asking for you."

"Not afraid that I'll talk, is he?"

"Why would he be afraid of that?"

"I dunno, but I think he is. That's why he fixed it with you to get me out of there. Well, if he is afraid, maybe we could do something to ease his mind."

"Like what?"

"Another twenty quid and I'd leave London, go north someplace."

"That's a rorty idea. But the captain had a better one."

"What's that?"

"This."

Pulling a knife from under his jacket, he stabbed Macy in the left side of the chest with surgical deftness. Macy stood there for a moment, frowning—as if he didn't know what had happened to him—then his knees gave way, and he collapsed on the wet stone paving. Whistling, Pollard wiped the knife on Macy's jacket and put it away. Picking up bricks and small loose stones, he began putting them in Macy's pockets so his body would sink when he tipped it into the river. He was reaching for more stone when he heard the sound of slow, heavy footsteps coming along Wapping High Street. He turned and saw a bulky shape topped with a constable's helmet silhouetted against the light from the pub. He froze, waiting. Then, as the constable heard or saw something and started down toward him, Pollard slipped away into the darkness.

10

The Colonel Is Outraged

The same footman opened the door when Wyatt and Tucker arrived at the embassy the next morning, and the same imposing majordomo was standing by.

"Good morning," said Wyatt pleasantly. "I'm afraid I don't know your name."

"It's Branza, Inspector," said the majordomo with a bow. "You wished to see the first secretary?"

"If he's here."

"He is, and Captain Benesh is with him. I believe they are expecting you. I will inquire."

He knocked at the door of the first secretary's office, went in and, a moment later, came out indicating that Wyatt and Tucker were to go in.

The colonel was at his desk and, as Branza had indicated, Captain Benesh was there also, leaning against one of the bookcases and smoking a long, thin cigar.

"Good morning, Inspector," said Katarov. "We were not sure what time you would be here, but I am afraid we have bad news for you. Or rather, no news at all—which I fear you will take as bad news."

"You're talking about George Vickery?"

"Yes. We have been in touch with the Bucharest police, and they have no record of his having arrived there, of his having registered at any hotel, or of anything having happened to him. I am afraid that the telegram Mrs. Vickery received was a hoax."

"That's a little hard to understand since, as I told you, our Post Office assures us it was sent from Bucharest."

"I'm not saying it was not sent from there. All I am saying is that no one in Bucharest seems to know anything about George Vickery."

"Well, let's forget about that for a moment. What about your coachman, Zachariah Macy?"

"We have not forgotten that you wished to talk to him, but for some reason he has not come in yet. As soon as he does, we will of course send him to see you."

"I'm afraid that's going to be rather difficult. You see, he's dead."

"He's what?"

"Dead. He was knifed sometime last night; his body was found on a dock near the Thames." Then, speaking very quietly and pleasantly, "When we asked for him yesterday, you said he wasn't here, but he was."

"What do you mean, he was?"

"I mean he was here when we asked for him and when Captain Benesh supposedly went looking for him."

"Are you suggesting that Captain Benesh did not really look for him?"

"I don't know. All I know is that he left several minutes after Sergeant Tucker and I did—left very unobtrusively by the rear, service entrance in a four-wheeler that was brought there specifically for that purpose."

"I know nothing about that," said Katarov emphatically. "Nothing at all. Do you, Captain Benesh?"

"Certainly not!"

"I was afraid of that," said Wyatt with an unhappy sigh. "In that case, could we talk to Stub Pollard?"

"Who?"

"Stub Pollard. A slight, dark chap who walks with a decided limp. He is a well-known cat burglar and served two sentences for robbery before he fell from a roof and broke his leg."

"And what makes you think he is here?"

"Sergeant Tucker and I both saw him leaving here yesterday soon after we had been here. It was he who brought the four-wheeler to the embassy's rear door when Macy left so suddenly and quietly. And Pollard himself left by way of the rear entrance at about ten o'clock last night and returned after midnight."

"It sounds to me, Inspector," said Katarov with obvious restraint, "as if you have been keeping a very close watch on the embassy."

"Oh, we have," said Wyatt cheerfully. "Very close."

"Do you mind telling me why?"

"Not at all. I told you that we are very concerned about George Vickery, who disappeared about a week ago in Bucharest. What I did not tell you was that we are even more concerned about his three-year-old son, Michael, who was kidnapped from his home in Somerset six days ago and brought here to London."

Tucker, following Wyatt's instructions to watch Benesh, saw him stiffen and then force himself to relax.

"Are you suggesting, Inspector," said Katarov with dangerous calm, "that someone here at the embassy had something to do with that?"

"Let me tell you what else we know, Colonel, and see if that answers your question. We know that Zack Macy drove the hired carriage in which the boy was taken from his house in Somerset to Bath. We know that Macy came down to London with two other people and engaged the cab that took them from Paddington to some unknown destination. Doesn't it seem logical to you that the reason he left here so abruptly was because he didn't want to be questioned as to the whereabouts of the boy? And the reason he was killed was because someone wanted to make sure that he never *could* be questioned?"

"That does not answer my question, Inspector. I repeat: are you suggesting that someone here—and by that I mean someone who is here in an official capacity—had something to do with the criminal action of which you have just told us?"

"There's a simple way in which you can prove that no one here did, Colonel. Give us permission to search the embassy and convince ourselves that the boy is not here."

"That," said the colonel, striking the desk with sudden violence, "is the most outrageous thing I have ever heard! You insult us by implying we have been involved in criminal behavior—and then suggest that we exonerate ourselves by asking for something that is a violation of our diplomatic immunity! I must ask you to go, sir—go and not come here again! And you may be sure that I shall make the strongest representations about this to your Foreign Office!"

"By all means do so, Colonel," said Wyatt bowing politely. "Good morning to you. And to you too, Captain," he said to Benesh. Then, with Tucker beside him, he walked casually and unhurriedly out of the room and across the entrance hall. The footman opened the door and, still with no haste, the two policemen went down the three steps.

It was only when they had turned left and were walking up Court Street that Tucker said, "Well, well, Inspector, aren't you ashamed?"

"Should I be?"

"Indeed you should. You gave him a chance to make one of the most highfalutin' speeches I've heard since the Gaiety Theatre burned down, and what do you say in answer? You, not a blinking foreigner, but an Englishman, a descendant of Shakespeare. 'Good morning to you.' "

"What should I have said? 'Thy conscience hath a thousand several tongues and every tongue brings in a tale and every tale condemns you for a villain'?"

"Better. Much better. I watched Captain Benesh-Benson the way you told me to. And when you said the boy had been brought here to London, he twitched like he'd been jabbed with a sailmaker's needle."

"I know. I saw it."

"What do we do now?"

"What I thought we'd have to do. Let's go see friend Galt."

They continued up Court Street to the hotel. Mr. Galt, the heavyset, smiling owner was talking to one of the guests when they came in. He excused himself and came over.

"Good morning, Inspector . . . Sergeant. As you know, it'll be a while before The Footman opens. In the meantime, would you like some coffee?"

"You're very kind, Mr. Galt," said Wyatt. "I could use some coffee. But there's something else we'd like— something much more important."

"Oh?" said Galt, looking at him sharply. "You said you might want to set up a base here—a kind of command post. Is that what you mean?"

"It is."

"I told you that the writing room is almost never used. You're welcome to that."

"Thank you. It looks ideal. One more thing. I'd like to engage some rooms upstairs for as long as we stay here. A two-bedroom suite would do."

"Very good, Inspector. I'll tell the clerk."

"So you expect to be spending nights here as well as days," said Tucker as Galt went off.

"I think it's very likely, but I wasn't just thinking of myself. I suspect that when Mrs. Vickery hears what happened, she and Mrs. Wyatt will want to be closer to the scene of operations than St. John's Wood."

"I suspect you're right. Do you have any orders for me?"

"I will have. But let's go outside first, look over the terrain, and decide how we'll dispose our troops."

They went out, looking up the street toward the embassy, and Wyatt pointed out where he wanted men stationed.

"Well, here's a do," said Tucker, glancing past him. "You don't see many of them in this part of London."

Turning, Wyatt saw Jasper and Daniel Lee, the Gypsies he had last seen in the Somerset police station, coming toward them. And striking as they had been there, they were even more so in the drab London street. For they were dressed exactly as they had been when he last saw them.

"What are you doing here?" Wyatt asked.

"Why, looking for you, Inspector," said Jasper politely.

"Why?"

"You were there when the other inspector questioned us about our plans, and I promised to keep in touch with the police."

"I remember. But what he meant was for you to keep in touch with him, not with me."

"Is that so? I'm sorry I misunderstood. But, as you can see, I'm here now."

"Yes. How did you know where I was?"

"Why, we went to Scotland Yard, and they told us."

Wyatt turned to Tucker, who was looking at the Gypsy with interest and amusement.

"Never," said Tucker.

"I agree," said Wyatt. "No one at the Yard would tell you where I was."

"No? Then maybe they didn't have to. I told you that my mother was a *chovihani*, a witch."

"Yes, you did. That must be the answer," said Wyatt. Then, noticing where Jasper was looking, "Do you know what that building is?"

"Which one?" asked Jasper innocently. "That one? No. Except . . . isn't that the Rumanian flag?"

"Probably. That's the Rumanian Embassy."

"Is it?"

"Yes." He looked at Jasper closely, intently. "Who the blazes are you anyway?"

"You know. I gave you my name."

"You gave me *a* name."

"Well, one is as good as another. May I ask you a question, Inspector?"

"You can always ask. Whether I answer is something else again."

"That boy, the one who was stolen in Somerset, you haven't gotten him back yet, have you?"

"No. Why are you so interested in him?"

"You know why. We talked about it in the police station. The inspector there thought that we had taken him. Or at least had something to do with his being taken."

"I didn't think that."

"No, you didn't. You think he's there, in the embassy, don't you?"

"Why do you say that?"

"Because I know you're looking for him and you're here."

"Do you think finding him is the only case I've got on my books?"

"I'm sure you have others. But I still think he's important to you. One final question. We heard that the boy's mother came down to London with you. True?"

"Yes."

"How is she?"

"How do you expect a woman to be whose child has been kidnapped and who doesn't know what has happened to her husband?"

Jasper nodded slowly. "Yes," he said thoughtfully. He dropped his eyes, then looked up again. "Since we are here and not in Somerset, Inspector, may we keep in touch with you? May we stop in from time to time to see how this case is going?"

Wyatt did not answer immediately, but Tucker, who had learned to read him over the years, knew that a great deal was going on behind his steady gray eyes.

"Yes, Jasper," he said finally. "By all means stop by."

11

The Foreign Office Is Concerned

"Which building is it?" asked Verna.

It was that afternoon and they were looking out of the window of the hotel room Wyatt had engaged—Verna, Mrs. Vickery, Wyatt, Andrew, and Markham.

"That one," said Mrs. Vickery. "The white one with the flag, on the other side of the street."

"That's right," said Verna. "I forgot that you had been there."

"I was there twice to ask about my husband. And now you tell me that that is where my boy is," she said to Wyatt.

"Not exactly. I said there is a good chance that that's where he is."

"But you're not sure."

"No."

She nodded. She had not taken her eyes from the embassy since they had entered the room and was staring at it as if, by sheer force of will, she would be able to see through the walls.

"It was very thoughtful of you to let me come here," she said, "but there's still a great deal I don't understand."

"The extraterritoriality?" said Verna. "The diplomatic immunity?"

"No. I can see how an embassy must be protected just as a diplomat must and therefore you cannot just go in and search the place; but . . . if they did take him, why did they do it? Why do they want him? It's not as if they were criminals and want ransom."

"No," said Wyatt. "And I'm not absolutely sure why they do want him. But I have some ideas about it, and there are several things I am looking into."

"Things that may help us to get him back?"

"They may."

"Let me ask you this. What would happen if I went over there, told them who I was, and asked them if they had Michael?"

"What did they say when you asked them about your husband?"

"They said they knew nothing about him. That they did not believe he had ever gone to Bucharest."

"Do you think that's true?"

"No."

"In other words, they lied to you. If your boy is there, don't you think they'd lie to you about that too?"

"I suppose they would. Then there's nothing we can do except wait."

During all the time that she was talking, she never raised her voice, and somehow Andrew found this more affecting than if she had been shrill and hysterical. He looked at her—her pale, drawn face and her eyes that were dark with pain—and then looked away. A movement outside caught his eye.

"Wyatt, look!" he said.

Wyatt glanced at the four-wheeler that had drawn up in front of the embassy.

"Ah, yes. Please stay here," he said to Verna and Mrs. Vickery. "I'll be back soon." Walking quickly, he went out.

Andrew glanced at Markham. Wyatt hadn't said anything about them, so they hurried out, too. They went down the stairs and had just reached the street outside the hotel when the door of the embassy opened and Captain Benesh came out with a lady on his arm. He was in full fig, wearing a top hat, striped trousers, and a frock coat, and she was all in black, apparently in deep mourning, for a heavy veil covered her face. He helped her into the carriage, gave some instructions to the driver, and was about to get in himself when Wyatt and Sergeant Tucker strolled up.

"Good afternoon, Captain," said Wyatt politely.

"Good afternoon, Inspector," said Benesh shortly.

"May I ask where you are going?"

"What?" Benesh stared at him. "How dare you ask me that? What possible concern is it of yours where I go?"

"It's of great concern. Don't forget that one of your employees was murdered. I can do nothing about anything that happens inside your embassy, but I am responsible for anything that happens outside. Therefore I'd like to know where you are going so that I can, if it seems necessary, send a constable along to protect you."

"That is unnecessary. This is Madame Zorn, the wife of one of our attachés. She has just received word that her father died and I am taking her to Victoria Station so that she can return home to Rumania for the funeral."

"My sympathies, Madame Zorn," said Wyatt. He bowed to her, and she inclined her head. "How did she get this word?" he asked Benesh.

"How?"

"Yes. As you know, we've been keeping a close watch on the embassy—for your protection—and you received no telegrams today."

"No, we did not," said Benesh venomously. "But we got our mail, and the word came by letter. Does that satisfy you?"

"Of course."

"May we go then?"

"By all means." While Wyatt and Benesh were talking, Sergeant Tucker had gone around to the other side of the carriage where Madame Zorn was sitting and looked, first at her and then down.

"Thank you," said Benesh ironically. Getting into the four-wheeler, he slammed the door.

Tucker was now looking at Wyatt and apparently sending him a message for, as the driver shook the reins and prepared to drive off, Wyatt said, "Just a second. I'm not sure the other door is shut. Will you try it, Sergeant?"

"Yes, Inspector," said Tucker. He opened and shut the door. Then, apparently not satisfied, he reached inside to test the latch. When he did, Madame Zorn's veil must somehow have become entangled with the door handle. For when Tucker opened the door again—pulling on it hard and opening it wide—her veil was pulled off. Not only her veil, but the wig she wore underneath it, revealing the cropped hair, pasty face, and close-set eyes of Stub Pollard.

Pollard stared at Tucker for a moment, his mouth slightly open. Then despite his limp, he jumped out of the carriage and ran up the embassy steps so quickly that no one could have caught him if they had tried—though it must be admitted that neither Wyatt nor Tucker did try. Someone inside the embassy must have been watching, for the door opened and he slipped inside. But as he did, Andrew saw that the sole of one of his boots was built up so that it was much thicker than the other. That, of course, must have been what Tucker had seen.

Now Benesh jumped out of the four-wheeler also.

"Wait!" he said to the driver and, with a furious glance at Wyatt, he ran up the steps and into the embassy also.

"Well done," said Wyatt to Tucker.

"Thank you. I must say I rather liked it myself. You didn't want Pollard yet, did you?"

"No. I'd just as soon he stayed in there where he can worry them. One way or another, we'll pick him up when we're ready for him."

"Do you know what they want him for?" Markham asked Andrew under his breath.

"I think so," said Andrew. "I think they think that—under orders of course—he killed Zachariah Macy."

"Right you are, old sleuth," said Tucker. "We've already got two witnesses who saw him at The Eight Bells at the right time. When we're ready, we'll bring them face to face and make sure."

"Are you waiting for something?" Andrew asked Wyatt, who was standing negligently next to the four-wheeler.

"Yes," said Wyatt. "After all, they told the growler to wait."

The embassy door opened again, and this time Colonel Katarov came out. He was dressed as formally as Benesh had been, in a top hat and frock coat. His color high and his lips tight with suppressed rage, he bowed to Wyatt.

"Good afternoon, Inspector," he said. "I understand you wanted to know where Captain Benesh was going. Would you like to know where *I* am going? Or do you perhaps know?"

"I think I can make a fairly good guess," said Wyatt. "The Foreign Office."

"Exactly. My compliments. You will be here when I return with—I hope—someone of some importance?"

"I will be here."

"Excellent. Thank you. The Foreign Office on Whitehall," he said to the cabby and got into the four-wheeler. Tucker closed the door for him and turned to Wyatt as it drove off.

"Now that," he said, "was more like it. In fact, it was top-hole."

"I'm glad you liked it," said Wyatt.

"It seems to me," said Markham, "that if you're not besieging the embassy, you're doing the next thing to it."

"That's about it," said Wyatt. "I want them to know without any question that if the boy is in there, they're not going to be able to get him out."

"Will that help to get him back?" asked Andrew.

"I'm hoping it will keep them from hurting him. In the meantime, we'll be exerting pressure on them in other ways."

"Through the Foreign Office."

"Exactly."

"So that's why you weren't upset when the colonel said he was going to bring someone from there back here."

"I not only wasn't upset, I was delighted. As you probably guessed, I've been in touch with people there, and nothing would please me more than to have him bring someone back with him."

"Chadwick's father?"

"It's a good possibility. He's a Balkan specialist." He took out his watch and looked at it. "I'd say we have about a half hour before the next act begins, which should give us plenty of time to report to your mother and Mrs. Vickery on this one."

As usual, Wyatt's guess was a good one. It was just a little over a half hour later that the four-wheeler returned and drew up in front of the embassy. Katarov got out, followed by a somewhat younger man who, though dressed just as formally as the colonel, managed to look as casual as if he were on his way to play cricket.

Wyatt excused himself and went down the stairs, and Andrew and Markham followed him. Tucker, maintaining the police presence, stood in front of the embassy. When Katarov spoke to him, apparently asking for Wyatt, he pointed toward the hotel, indicating that he was coming.

"Hello, Chadwick," said Wyatt, strolling up to the new arrival.

"Oh, hello, Wyatt," said Chadwick, shaking hands with him. "Nice to see you again."

"You know each other?" said Katarov with some surprise.

"Oh, yes," said Chadwick. "We're both old Oxonians,

though I was there a few years before Wyatt. And, of course, we've had other dealings since then. The inspector has been extremely helpful in several important international matters; he's very highly thought of in our office."

Though this was all true, Andrew had a feeling that Chadwick was being a bit more fulsome than usual.

"I see," said Katarov. "Then since he is a friend of yours, perhaps he will explain to you what he has been unwilling to explain to me. And that is why he is harassing us and subjecting our every move—all our comings and goings—to such intense scrutiny!"

"But I have explained it," said Wyatt patiently. Then, turning to Chadwick, "Colonel Katarov cannot seem to understand that we are very concerned about his safety and that of all the members of the embassy."

"Safety. Why shouldn't we be safe here? What reason do you have to be concerned about us?"

"My dear colonel, have you forgotten that one of your employees was murdered?"

"You are talking about that coachman, Macy? But he was not killed here at the embassy. And he was not even a Rumanian!"

"No, he was not. But isn't it true that you sometimes have difficulty determining who is a Rumanian and who is not?"

"What do you mean? When have we had such a difficulty?"

"Captain Benesh had some difficulty with it just a short while ago. He claimed that the person in a veil whom he was escorting to Victoria Station was a woman, the wife of one of your attachés. But she turned out to be a man, a criminal whom we want to question about the murder of that coachman, Macy. And since I would not dream of accusing Captain Benesh of lying, it's clear that the man in the four-wheeler with him must have fooled him."

"Perhaps he did! But it is my conviction that it is you who are trying to fool me and Mr. Chadwick with half answers, half-truths."

"I'm sorry, Colonel," said Chadwick, "but I don't think that he's been trying to fool me or that he's been the least bit evasive. I wish you'd tell me precisely what it is that he hasn't told you."

"He has not told you the real reason he is watching the embassy so closely! He has not said a word about the boy who was kidnapped, whom we are supposedly hiding in the embassy! But now that I know you are a friend of his, I realize I cannot expect any action from you. So I shall take my protest to the highest possible authority—and I shall do that by way of Bucharest!"

And with a stiff bow, his face dark with anger, he stalked up the steps and into the embassy.

"Now that," said Chadwick thoughtfully, "is what I would call a ram-jam of a Rumanian rage."

"So would I. I have a feeling that I've gotten under his diplomatic skin."

"I agree. And since I'll probably have to answer a few questions about the matter, may I say I hope you know what you're doing?"

"You may. And I hope so, too," said Wyatt soberly.

"Then you're not quite as clear about it all as you appear to be?"

"I'm clear about what I'm hoping to accomplish. I told you, in the note I wrote you, about the child who had been kidnapped, didn't I?"

"You did. And said you thought he was being held at the embassy, but you didn't say why they wanted him."

"Because I don't know why, though I have some ideas. It might help if you told me exactly what was going on in Rumania right now."

"I'll tell you what I can, though I must confess we're not too clear on it ourselves. The fact is we're getting some strange and rather puzzling signals from Bucharest these days." He paused, looking at Andrew and Markham who had moved closer and were listening intently. "I see that the junior branch of the Yard is still with you."

"Yes," said Wyatt. "You know Tillett of course, who is a friend of your son's. And this is Markham, who's at school with both of them."

"How do you do, sir," said Andrew. "Would you mind if we listened, too?"

"Not at all," said Chadwick. "There's nothing secret about what I'll be saying—it's just confusing. What do you know about Rumania?"

"Not very much," said Andrew. "I believe they've had a difficult time for quite a while now—first with the Turks, then the Russians and Austro-Hungarians. It's only recently that things have settled down a bit."

"That sums it up fairly well. The present king is named Charles, and he's not a bad sort, inclined to be friendly to us in the west. He's getting on, however, and we always expected that his brother, Prince George of Moldavia, would take over after him. George was friendly to us also. But, about nine months ago, he died."

"Where did that leave things?"

"We're not sure. Prince George had two sons, Maximilian and John. Maximilian was supposedly even more friendly to us than his father, but they were on the outs because Maximilian married a commoner instead of someone who was properly royal."

"How does the king feel about him?"

"We gather the king has reservations about Maximilian too—because of the marriage and because he's been away a good deal. On the other hand, while the king likes Prince George's other son, John, quite a lot, the fact is that John isn't really George's son, but his stepson. You see, Prince George's first wife, Maximilian's mother—who was English, by the way—died about ten years ago and George then married the Countess Sylvia, who was a widow and already had a son, John."

"In other words, John is Maximilian's stepbrother and not actually in the succession."

"Exactly. As you can see, the situation is one of Balkan—which is to say, Byzantine—complexity."

"Yes, I can see that. What does the Rumanian ambassador have to say about it all?"

"Count Rozarin? I wish I knew. We like the old boy. He's intelligent, dedicated, democratic, and a good friend. But, as you've probably heard, he's been very ill—so ill that no one can get to see him."

"You've tried?"

"Several times. We offered to send in one of our own doctors to look at him, but old Katarov and the others here won't have it. They say he's being taken care of and as soon as he's well enough, they'll let us know. But in the meantime we're very much in the dark."

"You are, and we are, too," said Wyatt. "And I have a feeling that's exactly where our friends at the embassy want us to be."

12

The Yard's Junior Branch

"You mean to say," said Sara, "that even though they're fairly sure that the boy is in there, no one can go in and see if he is?"

"That's right," said Andrew.

"It doesn't make sense," she said flatly.

"Maybe not," said Markham, "but that's the way it is. They know for a fact that Stub Pollard, a known criminal and probably a murderer, is in there, and they can't do anything about that either."

"Well, as I said, it doesn't make sense," said Sara, who had joined them at the hotel as soon as she got out of school.

"But it does," said Andrew. "All diplomacy is based on the principle that the diplomat cannot be arrested or injured in any way. If this weren't so, no two nations would ever be able to discuss things with one another.

And once you give immunity to a diplomat, you've got to extend it to the place where he works and lives."

"All right," said Sara. "I suppose I don't like it because I don't like what's happening. Bad people are using a good rule for bad purposes."

"Unfortunately that happens fairly often," said Andrew. "Hello," he added, glancing up the street. "I wondered what you were looking at," he said to Markham.

"Your stepfather said they were here," said Markham, "and I wondered if we'd see them."

"They're Gypsies, aren't they?" said Sara, who had turned and was looking with frank interest at the two men who were approaching them.

"Yes," said Andrew. Then, as the men paused, "Hello."

"Greetings," said Jasper. "I don't know your names, but we saw you before—at the police station in Medford."

"That's right. I'm Andrew Tillett. This is Christopher Markham. And this is our good friend, Sara Wiggins."

"It's a pleasure to meet you," said Jasper formally. "I'm Jasper Lee and this is Daniel Lee."

"Are you brothers?" asked Sara.

"I could answer that by saying, 'Aren't all men brothers'? And even if that isn't true, I could observe that most Gypsies are related in some way. But the truth is, no. We are not brothers, not related. We are merely, as you claim you are, good friends." Then, looking at each of the three young people in turn, "Am I right in assuming you have some special interest in this case?"

"What case do you mean?" asked Andrew.

"I think you know. The case of the boy who was taken from the house in Medford. You were there, in the police station with that Scotland Yard inspector, Wyatt. And you're here now."

"Yes," said Andrew. "And we do have a special interest in the case. Markham and I are at school in Medford and, without meaning to, were involved in the kidnapping. But besides that, Inspector Wyatt, who's in charge of the case, is my stepfather."

"We thought you were involved in some way. I was impressed by the fact that the inspector knew some Romany. A good policeman, I think."

"The best one in Scotland Yard," said Sara stoutly. "The best one in England and probably the best one anywhere."

"He certainly seems to have admirers," said Jasper, "which is always a good sign. Not that I needed such a sign. I liked him from the first time I saw him."

"You haven't told us why *you're* specially interested in the case," said Markham. "Why you've come all the way down here from Somerset."

"But you were there when we were told to keep in touch with the police."

"I think Inspector Gillian meant that you should keep in touch with him," said Andrew. "Not come down here to London."

"Perhaps we misunderstood," said Jasper. "And perhaps we wanted to come down here anyway. After all, in the beginning we were suspected of having been involved in the kidnapping, and we won't rest easy until our name is cleared." Then, as Andrew nodded sympathetically, "Have there been any new developments?"

"The first secretary at the embassy doesn't like what's been going on, the way the police have been stopping everyone who tries to leave the embassy, and he brought someone from the Foreign Office to make them stop. But the inspector convinced the man from the Foreign Office that he was doing what they were doing to protect the Rumanians."

"I see. And are you still not sure—really sure—that the boy is in there, in the embassy?"

"No. The inspector thinks he is, but he's not sure."

"And if he *were* sure?"

"I think he'd do something," said Sara. "I don't know what, but he'd do something."

"Yes," said Jasper. "I have a feeling he'd do something, too. And the woman—the boy's mother—how is she?"

"About the way you'd expect. If she didn't have faith in the inspector also—*and* if she didn't have Andrew's mother to talk to—I don't know what she'd do."

"Yes," said Jasper. "I can imagine what it must be like."

Daniel, his companion, said something to him in their own tongue, and Jasper turned, looking up the street.

"Ah," he said as Benesh came out of the embassy.

"Someone seems to be leaving the sanctified precincts. Do you know him?"

"Yes," said Andrew. "That's Captain Benesh, the first secretary's aide. Tucker!" he called.

"You don't have to call me," said Tucker, coming out of the hotel. "We've been expecting something like this. Good afternoon, friend Jasper. Good afternoon, friend Daniel."

"Good afternoon, Sergeant," said Jasper. "What have you been expecting?"

"That someone would be going off to send a telegram to Bucharest. But we'll soon see," he said as a uniformed constable fell into step behind Benesh and followed him, making no attempt to disguise his purpose.

"And if he does send a telegram?" said Jasper.

"We'll get a copy of it. It will probably be in code, but with a little help, we'll be able to decode it."

"Of course," said Jasper. "The good inspector continues to impress me. Is he inside?"

"No," said Tucker. "He's at the Yard looking into some new information that's just come in. But he'll be back this evening."

"Then I shall return at that time also. It is very important that I see him." Again Daniel said something to him in their own tongue—it was hard to tell if it was a question or a statement—and Jasper shook his head impatiently. "I will wait no longer," he said firmly. "Good-bye, Sergeant," he said to Tucker. "Good-bye, my young friends," he said to Sara, Andrew, and Markham, and he went off, walking grimly and so quickly that Daniel almost had to run to keep up with him.

"I wish I knew what his game is, why he's got his spoon in this pot," said Tucker, looking after him. "His nibs seems to know; he says they're on our side, so I guess they are."

"I'm sure they are," said Sara. "He was asking about Mrs. Vickery."

"That poor lady," said Tucker. "She looks as if she hasn't closed her eyes since she came down to London. Enough to break your heart, it is."

"We know," said Sara.

"I've asked our friendly proprietor for some tea," said Tucker. "If you want some, come inside."

"In a little while," said Andrew. Then, as Tucker went back into the hotel, "Well? Anyone got anything to say?"

"No," said Sara. "But a tenner to a tanner, you have."

"How do you know?"

"I've had a feeling about it ever since I saw you at breakfast."

"Well, you're right. I didn't want to say anything about it then. I thought I'd wait until you got here this afternoon. But while Mrs. Vickery's been wonderful—courageous and patient and all that—I don't think she can take much more. And I'm not sure I can either. So I think it's time we did something."

"You mean you have an idea about something we *can* do?" said Markham.

"Yes."

"Tell us," said Sara.

"It's not a dead sure thing," said Andrew. "There's lots that can go wrong with it, but here's what I had in mind."

They were silent for a long moment when he had finished.

"You're right when you said that things can go wrong," said Sara thoughtfully. "Quite a few things can. But at the same time, I think it's worth a try."

"So do I," said Markham. "I'm going to be in on it, am I not?"

"Yes, I suppose so," said Andrew. "You can get what we need for the first part, can't you, Sara? Clothes and makeup?"

"Of course. You were planning to do it tonight?"

"Yes. The sooner the better."

"I agree. And there are any number of places I can get what we need—not that we're going to need much."

"There's just one thing," said Markham. "I'd like to be the one who goes in."

"Nothing doing!" said Andrew. "It was my idea."

"I know. But you see, I couldn't do the first part. I'm not sure enough of myself, wouldn't be able to play along with Sara the way you can. On the other hand, I can do the rest easily. I'm smaller than you are and I'm quick and . . . please!" he said as Andrew began shaking his head. "You've got to let me do it! After all, I'm responsible for what happened. If it weren't for me and my stupidity, it never would have happened. Won't you please let me do it?"

"It could be dangerous," said Andrew seriously. "They're a bad lot, and there's no telling what they might do if you're caught."

"I know. But I don't care. I'm not saying I'm as brave or clever as you, but I'm sure I can manage."

"It's not a matter of being brave or clever. I'd be scared to death if I did it. But I am a little older than you are, and. . . ." He turned to Sara. "What do you think?"

She had been studying Markham. Now she nodded.

"If he wants to do it, I think we should let him. He'll be all right."

"Thank you, Sara!" said Markham fervently. "Thank you very much!"

13

Inside the Embassy

Aristide Denon, pastry chef of the Rumanian embassy, was in a bad mood. There was nothing surprising about that. He had been at the embassy for about six weeks, and he had been in a bad mood for most of the time. How could he help it when day after day he had to work in the same kitchen with Zelescu, that idiotic Rumanian, who had the effrontery to call himself a chef?

But today had been worse than usual. Partly, of course, it was because of what had happened at lunch. For the third time in two weeks, Zelescu had prepared *mamaliga*, that ridiculous national dish, and had gotten furious when Aristide said that, if no one minded, he would make himself an omelette instead. But most of Aristide's irritation was due to the fact that he was making puff pastry—for which he had always been famous—and it was not coming out as it should. And why wasn't it coming out?

"It's the flour," he had explained to his wife. "A dozen times I have said to Zelescu, 'Get me some French flour and some butter from Normandy and I will make you pastry so light it will float in the air.' But does he? No! 'I use what I can get here in London,' he says. 'And you must do the same.'"

Muttering, Aristide folded the puff pastry dough, rolled it out, and was folding it again when he heard the door that opened on to the mews open and close.

He turned with an angry scowl, for a draft now could make his puff pastry heavier than ever.

"*Que veux tu?*" he said to the two children who stood there awkwardly and uncomfortably looking at him. "Who are you and what you want?"

"Please, sir," said the girl in a rather nasal voice. "We're looking for our father."

"Your fahzer? He works here?"

"Yes, sir."

"What he do?"

"He's a dishwasher, sir."

"A dish . . . ?" Then as she did a very creditable imitation of someone washing dishes. "Oh, *un plongeur.*"

He looked at her more closely. In spite of her ragged dress, bare feet, and dirty face, there was something appealing about her. She looked at him directly with bright, intelligent eyes and her smile was charming. As for the boy with her, though his clothes were ragged and his face was dirty, too, he seemed quite sturdy and manly.

"*Eh bien,*" he said. "Come, we will look for him." He put down his rolling pin and was drying his hands on his apron when Zelescu came storming up.

"What this?" he shouted, for he never talked in a normal voice. "Who these? Where they come from?"

"First," said Aristide, "please to speak like a person, not bellow like a bull!"

"What?"

"I ask you again, as I ask you a dozen times before, please to lower your voice when you speak to me!"

"And I ask you again, who these are?"

"If you have eyes, you can see that they are children!"

"So?"

"They are looking for their fahzer."

"What fahzer? Who fahzer? There is no fahzer here!" And taking the girl by the shoulder, he turned her around and pushed her toward the door.

"Take your hands off her!" the boy said angrily.

"You talk to me, no-good?" said Zelescu.

"He talk to you—and I talk to you, too!" said Aristide. "I always know you are not a cook. Now I know you are not even a man! You are a monster—a barbarian without heart or feeling! How dare you so treat an innocent child?"

"I am no cook? No cook—I, Zelescu who have cooked for kings and princes? I spit on your Frenchness!" He did. "I cut you into cutlets!" And picking up a long butcher's knife, he advanced on Aristide, brandishing it like a cutlass.

"Ah, you want fight?" said Aristide. "Good. We fight!"

Reaching behind him with his left hand, he picked up the puff pastry he had been folding and with a graceful swing, slapped Zelescu in the face with it. Then he picked up his rolling pin and, as Zelescu snorted and tried to pull the sticky dough from his eyes and nose, Aristide struck him smartly across the knuckles with the rolling pin, knocking the knife from his hand.

"You make me like a cutlet, hein? I make you flat like a crêpe!" And he was raising the rolling pin again when the other kitchen door burst open and Captain Benesh came hurrying in.

"What's going on here?" he said. "Denon, no! Stop!" And catching the pastry chef's arm, he prevented him from bringing down the rolling pin with lethal force.

"Let me go! Let me go!" said Aristide. "I crack him like a walnut!"

"You'll do nothing of the sort!" said Benesh. "Stop it and behave!" Then seeing the two children, "Who are they, and what are they doing here?"

"They are looking for their fahzer," said Aristide. "He is *plongeur*—dishwasher."

"Do any of you know these children?" said Benesh, turning to the rest of the kitchen staff—underchefs and and sauciers, kitchen boys and dishwashers—who stood around staring with varying degrees of astonishment and amusement. "Is any one of you their father?" Then, when all shook their heads, "So. You have made a mistake. Out!" he said, shooing them toward the door.

"But that ain't so, guv'ner," said the girl. "I'm sure this is right. Ain't this the Viscount Dugdale's house?"

"No, it's not," said Benesh, opening the back door. "Out with you! Go on, out!" and pushing them out into the darkness of the mews, he slammed the door.

By picking their time carefully, moving quickly and quietly when the constables who watched the rear of the embassy were being relieved, Sara, Andrew, and Markham had been able to slip in the back door unobserved. But there was no way they could repeat that performance now. The embassy door had barely closed behind them when one of the constables was on them, taking each of them firmly by the arm.

"Hello," he said. "Who are you?"

"We're nobody," said Sara in her best Cockney whine. "We're just looking for our da. He works around here somewhere."

"Oh? Well, let me take a look at *you*." And whistling to the other constable to alert him, he took Sara and Andrew along the alley toward the street where a gaslight glowed in the growing darkness.

Meanwhile, where was Markham? The purpose of Sara and Andrew's diversion had been to give him a chance to get inside the embassy and hide. As soon as they were inside the door—before the pastry chef noticed them—Markham had seen what they had hoped to find, a flight of stairs that led to the embassy's upper floors.

Tapping Sara's arm to show her where he was going, Markham ran over to the stairs and hurried up them. He paused at the top of the first flight. He could hear raised voices in the kitchen but could not tell what was being said, what was going on. There was a door on the other side of the landing. He opened it carefully and looked out. It opened on to a corridor with doors on both sides. Was what he was looking for behind one of them?

He hesitated. Then recalling that he, Sara, and Andrew had decided that the best procedure was to start at the top and work down, he went up another flight. There was another door there and, when he opened it, he found himself looking at another corridor, but one that looked much less elegant than the one on the floor below.

He started to go out, then paused. His heart was pounding with fear. He had been brave enough when he had told Andrew that he wanted to be the one to go into the embassy. At least he had *sounded* brave. The truth was that he had been afraid then, too, but not as afraid as he was now. Because now he was in the embassy, where he had no right to be; and though no one had seen him yet, once he started opening doors and looking into rooms, wasn't there a good chance that someone would see him? And if they did, what would they do to him? He didn't know, and he forced himself not to think about it. Because, frightened as he was, he had to go out and look into those rooms. Knowing that the longer he waited, the harder it would be to leave the shelter of the stairwell, he opened the door all the way and stepped out into the corridor.

He pressed his ear against the nearest door and listened. He could hear nothing. He tried the knob—the door wasn't locked—and he pushed it open and looked in. It was a simple, severe room with one bed in it, and it was empty. He closed the door and went to the next one. That was a bedroom, too, and that was empty also. The next two were offices, but like the bedrooms, they were empty at the moment.

In the middle of the corridor there was another stairway, an open one that must have been the main stairway. When he looked down, he saw that it rose from the entrance hall just opposite the front door.

A footman stood just inside the front door. And from a distance came the clink of silver and china and the low buzz of voices. That was why he hadn't seen anyone in the upper stories of the embassy. It was dinnertime, and everyone was at their evening meal in either the main dining room or in the servants' dining room.

Moving with more assurance, he looked in the rest of the rooms on the top floor. One was a storeroom, the rest were bedrooms, and they were all empty.

He returned to the backstairs, went down a flight, and came out into the corridor on the floor below. There were only a few doors on this floor, and when he opened the first one, he saw why. This was a bedroom, too, but it was much larger than the ones on the floor above. It had a sofa in it as well as two beds and was probably for visiting dignitaries. Like the ones above, there was no one in it but, whereas some of the ones on the floor above had clothes scattered about, this one was completely empty.

He went out and was about to try the next room when he heard the clink of dishes and the sound of footsteps coming up the main stairs. He returned hurriedly to the backstairs and shut the door, but not all the way. He left it open just a crack so that he could see out.

An elderly woman in what appeared to be a nurse's uniform, except that she did not wear a cap, appeared at the top of the stairs carrying a tray. Bracing the tray against her hip, she took out a key, unlocked the door of the room next to the one Markham had just been in, went in, and shut the door after her.

A nurse carrying a tray. The ambassador, he recalled, was supposed to be ill—so ill that he could not be seen. Was that who was in the room? But then why was the door kept locked? Was it so that he would not be disturbed? That seemed unlikely. Besides, there did not seem to be much food on the tray—not enough for a grown man. Unless he was so ill that he could only eat sparingly. All in all, it seemed to be something that should be looked into.

Opening the door, he listened for a moment to make

sure no one else was coming up the stairs, then hurried along the corridor to the room he had just been in, went in, and closed the door.

Going to one of the windows, he looked out. The room he was in and the one next to it were in the rear of the embassy, facing the mews rather than the street. It was not more than six or eight feet from one window to the other and, more important, there was a sturdy metal downspout between them. He had noticed that and the fact that ivy covered most of the rear wall of the embassy as he, Sara, and Andrew had waited to run into the mews and enter the embassy's rear door. He had noticed it because he was quite a good rock climber—it was one of the things he enjoyed doing when he was at school—and it had occurred to him that if they could not get into the embassy any other way, he could climb up the downspout.

Now, opening the window, he stepped out and stood on the window ledge. Holding on to the top of the window, he stretched out a foot and found he could easily reach one of the metal brackets that held the downspout to the brick wall. He tested it, putting more and more of his weight on it. Finding it was strong, he transferred his hand grip from the window to the downspout and swung over to the bracket. Now he stretched a foot out to the window ledge of the room he had seen the nurse go into and leaned over slowly until he could look in.

In the darkness outside he could make out only the

shapes of large objects, like the downspout. But a gaslight was burning in the room, and by its light he could see the nurse standing in front of a bed. She turned aside to take something from the tray, and when she did, he saw that she was feeding—not an old man—but young Michael Vickery.

The boy was either very sleepy or he had been drugged, for his eyes kept closing, and the only way the woman could get him to eat was by actually putting the spoon in his mouth. But, apart from that, he seemed well.

Releasing his hold on the side of the window, Markham swung back to the drainpipe. Now that he had found what he had hoped to find, he could not wait to tell Sara, Andrew, and anyone else who might be interested. And so, instead of going back into the empty room and leaving the way he had come in, he started down the downspout, stepping on a bracket when there was one, and sliding when there wasn't. He went down as quickly and quietly as he could, but he must have made more noise than he realized for, as he dropped the last few feet to the cobblestones that paved the mews, a large hand reached out and took him firmly by the collar of his jacket.

14

Jasper Again

Sitting at one of the desks in the writing room of the Court Street Hotel, Wyatt was going over Tucker's notes on what had happened that afternoon. He looked up as Jasper came in, followed by his companion Daniel.

"I've been expecting you," said Wyatt. "Tucker told me you were here this afternoon and said you'd be back."

"Yes," said Jasper. "Is there anything new?"

"If you mean, do we have the boy back yet, the answer is no."

"I did not mean that," said Jasper. "If you had him back, you wouldn't be sitting there being sarcastic. I meant, have you been able to find out if he really is in the embassy?"

"No. But I found out several other things that I think

are interesting—things I would like to discuss with you, as a matter of fact."

"What sort of things?"

"I think you can guess," said Wyatt.

"Perhaps I can," said Jasper. "But I don't think this is the time to go into them."

"No? When is the time?"

"When you get the boy back. In the meantime—" He broke off as a constable came into the writing room with Sara and Andrew. He was holding each of them by the arm and, though he released them once they were in the room, he stood behind them to make sure they did not try to run away.

"What's this?" said Wyatt.

"Caught them coming out of the embassy, sir," said the constable. "Out the rear entrance on the mews. You said you wanted anyone coming out intercepted and brought here." ·

"Yes," said Wyatt. He looked at them—at Sara's bare feet and torn dress, at Andrew's ragged shirt and pants, and at both their carefully dirtied faces—and his face became stony. "You were in the embassy?" he said in a voice he was clearly trying hard to keep quiet and level.

"Yes," said Andrew.

"How did you get in?"

"Sneaked in the back way."

Wyatt glanced at the constable, then at Andrew again.

"Why?" he asked.

"Do you trust us?" asked Sara.

"Trust you?" said Wyatt, slamming his fist down on the desk. "I certainly don't trust you! When we first came to London from Somerset, I told you that while Andrew and Markham had been involved in the early stages of the case—responsible, in a sense, for what happened— you were all—and by all, I meant you too, Sara—to stay out of it and not to interfere in any way! Because it was both dangerous and politically sensitive. And what do you do? From what Constable Butts tells me—and from the way you look—you've not only been interfering, but you've actually been inside the embassy, the place that is our greatest problem at the moment!"

"If you said you did trust us," said Sara with dignity, "then I was going to ask you please not to ask us any questions. But since you *don't* trust us, even if you do ask them, we're not going to answer them."

"What?" said Wyatt. "Of all the distorted, perverted reasoning I ever heard of, that takes the biscuit!"

"If you will not answer the inspector's questions, will you answer one for me?" said Jasper.

"I don't know," said Sara. "What is it?"

"Did you go in there—into the embassy—because you thought the missing boy might be in there?"

Sara hesitated for a moment, looking at him. Then she nodded. "Yes," she said.

"And was he there?"

"We don't know. We were just in the kitchen."

"Ah!" said Jasper. "But you think he might be in there. And if you think so, then *he* must think so, too." He nodded toward Wyatt. "Even though he will not admit it. You do think so, don't you?" he said to Wyatt.

"I think it's very possible," said Wyatt.

"Do you think he's been hurt or harmed in any way?"

"I hope he hasn't been, no matter *where* he is."

"Would it make your task easier if I could guarantee that nothing *will* happen to the boy?"

"How can you do that?" asked Wyatt.

"You will see," said Jasper. Sitting down at one of the other writing desks, he took a sheet of paper from the rack that held the hotel stationery, picked up a pen, and began to write.

"No!" said Daniel, hurrying over to him. "Please!" He put his hand on Jasper's arm, trying to restrain him while he spoke to him with great passion in Romany or whatever language he had spoken to him before.

Jasper pushed him away and, when he persisted, spoke to him with such authority that Daniel drew back, stiffened, and finally bowed.

"Is there any sealing wax here?" asked Jasper, still writing.

"What?"

"Sealing wax. For sealing letters."

"I don't know," said Wyatt, looking in the drawer of the desk at which he was sitting. Sara and Andrew, intrigued, looked in the drawers of the other desks, and Sara finally found a small stub of it. She brought it to Jasper, who had now finished his note and put it in an envelope.

"Thank you," he said. "Match," he said to Daniel. Daniel gave him a match; Jasper struck it, heated the stick of sealing wax until it was soft, then, reaching inside his shirt, took out a ring that he wore on a string around his neck and pressed it into the wax, sealing the letter.

"Would you have one of your constables take this to the embassy and give it to the first secretary?" he said, handing the letter to Wyatt. "If he is asked who gave it to him, he is to say he doesn't know, but that he was told to wait for an answer."

Wyatt looked at him, at the impression the ring had made in the red wax, then nodded.

"Do it," he said, giving the note to Tucker. Tucker saluted, went outside, and spoke to one of the constables who was on duty outside the hotel.

The constable walked with a policeman's measured pace to the embassy and rapped the brass door knocker. Branza, the white-haired majordomo, opened the door, and the constable gave him the note. The majordomo took it, glanced at the seal, and went inside, closing the door behind him.

A minute went by, two minutes. By the light of the gaslight that was almost directly overhead, Wyatt and the others in the hotel writing room could see the constable standing patiently in front of the embassy door. Then the door opened again, and Colonel Katarov came out with the letter in his hand.

"Who gave you this?" he asked sharply.

"Sergeant Tucker," said the constable.

"And where did he get it? Where is the man who wrote it?"

"I don't know, sir. All I know is that Sergeant Tucker told me to give it to you and wait for your answer."

"I see," said Katarov. He looked at the constable, then up the street at the hotel, which he knew Wyatt was using as his command post. "Very well. Tell the man who wrote the letter that there is someone else I must consult. I will do that immediately by telegraph. But in the meantime, tentatively, we agree."

"Yes, sir," said the constable. And saluting, he turned and walked with the same unhurried pace back to the hotel, where he repeated what Katarov had said to Wyatt, Jasper, and all the others in the writing room.

"Do you know whom he must consult?" Wyatt asked Jasper.

"Yes."

"How long will it take?"

"It is evening now, but he should hear before noon tomorrow."

"And in the meantime?"

"We wait, and you continue your watch on the embassy. But at least we know that the boy is safe."

"If you trust them, yes," said Wyatt.

"You mean you do not trust them?"

"I don't know. There are times when I don't trust anybody." He turned as the door of the writing room opened and another constable, the partner of the one who had caught Sara and Andrew, came in holding Markham by the collar of his jacket.

"Here's another one, sir," he said to Wyatt. "The other two came out the back door. But this one, he came down the drainpipe like a blinking Barbary ape."

"You were in the embassy, too?" said Wyatt.

"Yes, sir. Sara and Andrew went in first and created a diversion so I could slip in and go upstairs."

"You *did* go upstairs?"

"Yes, sir."

"Why?"

"To see if the Vickery boy was there." He paused. "And he is."

"You mean you saw him?"

"Yes, sir. He's in the big room at the top of the stairs— the one the ambassador is supposed to be sick in."

"You're sure about that?" said Jasper with great intensity. "You saw him with your own eyes?"

"Yes, sir."

"Thank you! I won't forget this!" And, his face alight,

he ran out of the writing room, across the hotel lobby, and out into the street.

"Jasper! Wait a minute, you impatient fool!" called Wyatt. "Where the devil do you think you're going?"

It was a question that required no answer. Running like a Rugby back who has scooped up a loose ball, Jasper was pounding up the street toward the embassy.

15

Reunion

Wyatt ran out of the hotel also, followed by Tucker, Daniel, and the three young people. But hard as they ran, they were not quick enough. Before they were anywhere near the embassy, Jasper had reached the door and was rattling the knocker, raising it and bringing it down again and again as rapidly and hard as he could. Andrew and the others could hear it from some distance off, and the clamor inside the embassy must have been deafening. By the time they ran up, Branza, the white-haired majordomo, was opening the door.

"Villainous rascal!" he said angrily. "What do you do? How dare you make so unseemly a noise?"

Pushing him aside so vigorously that he staggered and almost fell, Jasper ran past him and up the stairs. Hurrying in through the open door, Wyatt caught and steadied the elderly man. Then as Tucker, Daniel, and the three young people arrived, the door of the first secretary's office opened, and Colonel Katarov, startled by the thunder of the knocker, came storming out. He was asking indignant questions in Rumanian, but when he saw Wyatt, he switched to English.

"What are you doing here?" he said furiously. "How dare you come in here when I forbade you to do so? As for the rest of you, out! Get out and stay out!"

"Forgive me, Colonel," said Wyatt quietly. "You should know that I would not come in here without a good reason. And I have a very good one. We were following a man who might be very dangerous, hoping to catch him before he burst in here. But we were too late."

"It was he who used the door knocker that way?" Katarov asked Branza. And when the elderly majordomo nodded, "Where is he?"

But before Branza could answer, there was a loud noise from upstairs as Jasper drove his heel at the locked door. He did it again, and the door crashed open.

"Benesh!" called Katarov, and he said something rapid and excited in his native tongue. Benesh came hurrying into the entrance hall and, when Katarov repeated what he had said, he stiffened, took a revolver from a holster under his jacket, and started for the stairs. But as he reached the bottom step, he paused. For Jasper, with young Michael in his arms, was coming down the stairs.

"You!" said Katarov.

"Why are you surprised?" said Jasper. "You got my note."

"Yes. But I did not realize. . . . Stop! Stay where you are! Nothing has been settled yet! Stop or Benesh will shoot the boy!"

"You would not dare!"

"Would I not? You know what is at stake and what we have done so far! Do you think I would let anything—sheer sentimentality—stop me now? Benesh!"

This last was an order, and Benesh raised his revolver and aimed it at the boy. Jasper looked at him, down at the child whose eyes were closed, probably because of the drug he had been given, then up again.

"Yes," he said. "I suppose you would do it. You're quite capable of it."

"Indeed we are!" said Katarov. He turned his head. "Branza, get the boy, take him to my office, and stay with him until these intruders are gone.

The majordomo hesitated a moment, then bowed slightly.

"Yes, Colonel," he said.

He went up the first two steps of the stairs to where Jasper stood and held out his arms. Jasper, his face pale and set, held the boy tightly for a moment longer, pressing the blond head against his chest, then he placed the boy in Branza's arms.

Branza turned and, carrying the boy carefully, went

down the two steps to where Katarov and Benesh waited. Then, instead of going past them to Katarov's office, he kept walking in his usual controlled and almost stately manner toward the open door.

Katarov stared for a moment, unable to understand what was happening.

"Branza, wait!" he said. "What are you doing? Where are you going?" Then, as he realized what it meant, "Benesh, quick! Stop him!"

Benesh fired, and Branza stumbled. The bullet had hit him in the shoulder, and the blood welled out of the hole in his dark jacket and trickled down his back. But straightening up, he continued walking—out of the embassy door and into the street. Gun ready, Benesh ran after him. But the moment he stepped outside the door, Tucker clamped a huge hand on his wrist.

"Forgive me, sir," he said, quietly, taking the gun, in spite of Benesh's struggles. "What happens in your embassy may be your affair, but we do not permit guns in the streets of London."

Now Jasper ran down the last few stairs and out of the embassy. Tucker had tossed the gun to one of the constables and was holding up the wounded majordomo when Jasper reached them.

"Are you badly hurt, Branza?" he asked.

"I don't think so, Your Highness," he said. "Just my shoulder, but . . . you'd better take the boy."

"I will," said Jasper, taking the child back again. "And I'll not forget this. But why did you do it?"

"Why? I didn't know who he was, though I probably should have. But once I saw you and did know. . . ." He grimaced, his knees started to buckle, and he would have fallen if Tucker had not been holding him up.

By this time, Wyatt, Daniel, and the young people had joined them.

"Get him to a hospital right away," Wyatt said.

"Yes, sir," said Tucker. "Give me a hand, Beckett," he said to a constable, who put an arm around Branza, too, and began helping him up the street toward a four-wheeler that had been halted by the activity in front of the embassy.

"Is Mrs. Vickery at the hotel?" Jasper asked Wyatt.

"Yes."

Jasper went up the street and, noting the way he carried the child, Andrew suddenly realized something he should have realized before—why he had been so concerned about the boy.

Verna and Mrs. Vickery must have heard the shot and seen that something was going on in front of the embassy, because they were coming out of the hotel as Jasper and the others approached it.

Seeing the child, Mrs. Vickery stopped dead for a moment, then flew toward them.

"Is he all right?" she asked, holding out her arms.

"Yes," said Jasper, giving her the child.

"Are you sure?"

"Look," he said.

The child had been blinking sleepily during the last few minutes, opening his eyes, then closing them again. Now he opened them wide, looked up, and said, "Mummy."

"Michael!" she said. "Yes, he does seem to be all right. Oh, thank heaven! Thank . . ." For the first time she looked—really looked—at Jasper, and the color drained from her face.

"George!" she whispered.

"Yes, darling."

"But they said . . . they said. . . ."

"I know."

"Here," said Verna. "Give me the child."

She took the boy from his bewildered mother; and then Mrs. Vickery, sobbing, was in Jasper's arms, and he was kissing her and holding her as close as he had been holding the child.

"Well," said a drawling voice, "I seem to have come at a very opportune time." It was Chadwick.

"Yes," said Wyatt. "Very opportune."

"Boy all right?"

"Yes."

"Good." Then, with Foreign Office discretion, "I won't ask how you got him out."

"No, don't," said Wyatt. "Though actually it wasn't we who did it."

"Ah," said Chadwick. "And this is . . . ?" he asked, nodding toward Jasper.

"Yes," said Wyatt. Then as Jasper released Mrs. Vickery and glanced at them. "Your Highness," he said, "this is Blaine Chadwick of our Foreign Office. His Highness, Prince Maximilian George of Moldavia."

"Your Highness," said Chadwick, bowing.

"Mr. Chadwick," said Jasper, bowing in return.

"Prince?" said Mrs. Vickery. "I'm afraid you've made a mistake. This is my husband, George Vickery." Then her slight frown of surprise gave way to outright puzzlement. "But, George, why are you dressed that way? You look like a Gypsy."

"It's a long story, my dear," said Jasper. "And I'd just as soon not go into it in so public a place."

"I don't think you should," said Verna. "Let's go in there," she said, nodding toward the hotel. "Then you can not only be more private, but we can put young Michael to bed until we're ready to go back to our place."

16

A Royal Explanation

"How is he now?" asked Jasper as Mary Vickery came into the writing room some ten minutes later.

"Fine."

"Asleep?"

"Half asleep and half awake. One of the chambermaids is with him and I told him we'd both be up to take him home in a little while." Then, hurrying across the room to him, "I can't believe this, darling! To have both of you back again, you and Michael!"

"I know," said Jasper, embracing her. "Here, sit down."

He pulled out a chair and placed it next to the one Verna was sitting in.

"Thank you," she said, sitting. "Now tell me everything—where you've been, why you're dressed that way, and particularly why Inspector Wyatt called you Prince Something or Other."

"He did it because I am."

"A prince? But that's impossible!"

"No. I've often wished it weren't true. But I'm afraid it is."

"I don't understand."

"I'm not surprised. It's a complicated story." He looked at Wyatt, who sat on one of the desks near Chadwick and the young people. "How much do you know?"

"I guessed some things early on and discovered more of them later. But I certainly don't know everything, so I'd like to hear it all from the beginning."

"Very well. As the inspector indicated," he said to his wife, "I am Prince Maximilian George of Moldavia, nephew of King Charles of Rumania and next in line to the throne."

Mrs. Vickery still looked at him blankly. "But how is that possible? Aren't you British?"

"No. I'm Rumanian."

"But you haven't the slightest trace of an accent."

"My English is much better than my Rumanian, which my friend, Captain Dimitroff here," he nodded to the Gypsy who had called himself Daniel, "insists I speak with an English accent. The truth is that my mother was English—her father was the English ambassador—I had an English nurse from the beginning and was sent to school in England from the time I was ten."

"But why didn't you let anyone know who you were? Why did you call yourself Vickery?"

"It was my mother's name. She and my father agreed

that it would make things difficult for me to go to an English public school with a Rumanian name and title. So I used her last name and my second name, first at public school and then at Cambridge."

"All right. I can understand why you might do that to begin with. But why didn't you tell me the truth later on?"

"In the beginning, when we first met, I didn't think it mattered one way or another. Or rather, until I got to know you well, I wasn't sure whether you'd like me more with a title or less, so I decided to say nothing about it. Also, things were changing and I had another reason for keeping quiet about who I was."

"What do you mean?"

"When I was fourteen, my mother died. As you can imagine, that was a great loss to me because we had been very close. The following year, my father married again, this time—to the satisfaction of his brother, King Charles— he married a titled Rumanian lady."

"Countess Sylvia of Severin," said Chadwick.

"Yes," said Jasper, whom Andrew still had difficulty thinking of as a prince. "She was the widow of Count Nicholas of Severin, one of our oldest families, and she had a son, two years younger than I, named John. This began the change, because the countess did everything she could to drive a wedge between my father and me, telling my father that my studies should not be interrupted by the long trip home to Rumania and making me feel uncomfortable and out of place when I did go home."

"Didn't you realize what she was doing?" asked Wyatt.

"Yes, but I didn't care too much. I loved England, particularly later when I was married and had a child. And though I had been studying political economy because I thought it would be useful when I returned to Rumania, I began to think perhaps I wouldn't go back. That I would remain here. As a matter of fact, I was offered a post at Cambridge that I was considering. Then, about a year ago, my father died."

"Was that the telegram you received that upset you so much?" said Mrs. Vickery. "When you said something serious had happened and you had to go to Bucharest right away?"

"Yes. There was no time to tell you everything before I left, but I thought I would when I returned. Because, since King Charles had no children, when my father died, I became next in line for the throne."

"But you still didn't tell me," said Mrs. Vickery.

"No. Because while I was in Bucharest for my father's funeral, I began to realize something I should have been aware of long before. That my stepmother and stepbrother, Count John, were plotting against me—plotting to have John succeed to the throne instead of me."

"What made you realize it?" asked Chadwick.

"First of all, there was an attempt to kill me that I thought was an accident, but my friend, Mitya, here, assured me was not."

"I know was not," said Dimitroff. "I recognized driver of carriage that almost ran him down."

"Mitya is the son of my father's aide de camp and best friend," said the prince. "He began looking out for me the way his father looked out for my father. But the person who really made me understand what was going on was Count Rozarin, the Rumanian ambassador to England."

"Ah," said Chadwick. "We wondered about that. We always had great respect for the count."

"So did I. He was a good friend of my father—though he hadn't been able to get him to see what the countess was up to. He got me to see it very clearly, however, and we had a long talk about it. He advised me to return to England and let things go for a while to see if they would develop as we thought they might. It was when I realized that they were doing so—and developing very quickly—that I decided to leave Cambridge and move to Somerset. Because it became clear to me that if I was in danger, then Mary and my son might be also."

"But why didn't you tell me who you were then?" asked Mrs. Vickery.

"Partly because I didn't want to worry you—and partly for another reason I'll get to in a moment."

"Didn't the people you were concerned about, Count

John and those with him, know about your wife and child?" asked Wyatt.

"They knew about Mary. When we decided to get married, I asked my father to come to the wedding. But even though he admired the British and had married an Englishwoman himself, he was angry that I was marrying one also and refused to come."

"For political reasons?" asked Chadwick.

"Yes. His brother, the king, had been furious at him when he married my mother instead of someone connected with one of the royal families. That breach was only healed when my father married the Countess Sylvia. However, the king found out about my marriage, as did Sylvia and John; they found out about it and used it against me. However, my father had become quite ill by the time my son, Michael, was born and I saw no reason to upset him further, so I never told him."

"That means that no one knew about Michael until fairly recently," said Wyatt.

"I don't think anyone did until I went to Bucharest for my father's funeral. At that point I had become next in line for the throne and they must have looked into my marriage more carefully and discovered I had a son who would succeed to the throne after me. Then, about three weeks ago, I was summoned to Bucharest by the king. The day I got there, another attempt was made on my life."

"What sort?" asked Wyatt.

"Mitya and I were going out in the evening when someone shot at me."

"They fire three times," said Mitya. "One of the bullets go through the prince's hat before I am able to get him into cover."

"When I saw the king the next day, I told him about the attempts," said the prince, "told him I thought my stepbrother John was behind them, and he became furious at me, said I was saying that because I hated John. I told him that wasn't true, asked him to speak to Count Rozarin about it. He said he had summoned Rozarin to Bucharest at the same time he had summoned me, but the count had not yet arrived and no one knew where he was. But, when I pressed him, he agreed to another meeting in a day or so in which I could detail my charges against John."

"What happened at the meeting?" asked Chadwick.

"There was no meeting. I got word that it was to take place the following night on the king's yacht. A launch was sent to take Mitya and me out there. When we were about halfway to the yacht, the launch blew up."

"An accident?" said Wyatt.

"Do you think it was?"

"No."

"I'm sure it was not. The boatman was killed instantly. I was stunned and would have drowned if Mitya had not kept me afloat until I regained consciousness. We got to shore and decided that the best thing we could do would be to let everyone think we had died in the explosion and get out of Rumania."

"Was that when you disguised yourselves as Gypsies?" asked Andrew.

"Yes. Mitya had had a Gypsy nurse when he was a boy, and she and her whole family still feel as if he were her son. They gave us clothes and the false papers we needed to leave Rumania and get to England."

"What about that telegram I got saying that you had had an accident and were feared lost?" said Mrs. Vickery. "Did you send it?"

"No, my dear," said the prince. "The wreckage of the boat was found, and one of my friends who knew I was on it sent you the telegram."

"It's still too much for me," said Mrs. Vickery. "I still don't feel as if I've absorbed it all—not just what happened, but what it means."

"I know," said the prince. "And as far as that's concerned, I did something a little while ago that almost took care of that."

"What was that?"

"In spite of I say no," said Dimitroff, "he write a note to Katarov saying that if he gave back boy all safe, he will give up throne—how you say it?—abdicate."

"I thought that's what you were doing with that note," said Wyatt. "And I'm glad your offer never went into effect."

"So am I," said Chadwick. "Especially in the light of the most recent developments."

"What developments are those?"

"They're the reason I came here tonight," said Chadwick. "And I think you'll find them reassuring. You said that the king was angry because he did not know what had happened to Count Rozarin. Well, the fact is that the count was—and still is—in a hospital in Paris."

"Was he hurt?"

"There was an attempt made to assassinate him as there was to kill you. He was wounded and was unconscious for a while, but the doctors assure us that he will recover. Meanwhile, the French police caught the man who shot him, and he has been identified as someone very close to Count John. This news—and the news of what happened to you, the thought you had been killed—has apparently convinced the king that everything you said to him was true. As a result, Count John and his mother are being held under house arrest pending an inquiry, and Colonel Katarov, Benesh, and all of Count John's other supporters here in London have been ordered home."

"But then it's all over!"

"Yes, Your Majesty. That particular problem seems to be settled. But there are others, aren't there?"

"Yes," said the prince. "It's very clever of you to realize that."

"What does he mean?" asked his wife.

"I said there were several reasons why I didn't tell you

who I was. One was because of the way I thought you would feel. Has it occurred to you that as things stand, one day in the not too distant future, I will be—not Prince of Moldavia—but King of Rumania? Then you will become queen and Michael will be king after me?"

The color left his wife's face, and she sat there for a moment in silence.

"I hadn't thought of that," she said finally. "And I'm not sure I like the idea."

"I suspected you wouldn't. Some women would, of course, be thrilled at the idea of being a queen, but I didn't think you would be. And, to be honest, I wasn't sure I liked the idea of being king. In fact, when my father died, I was going to tell that to my uncle, suggest that perhaps we should discuss the whole matter of the succession. But before I could, I realized what my step-brother was doing."

"Trying to kill you."

"Yes. He would of course have been next in line for the throne if I had refused to accept it. But once I realized how unscrupulous he was, I began to have second thoughts about the matter."

"Yes," said his wife. "I can see that."

"So we're back to the original dilemma. How do you feel about the prospect of my becoming king? Do you accept it? Can you accept it?"

"I don't know. I don't know what to say."

"Excuse me," said Dimitroff suddenly and vehemently. "I understand why you no want to say, but *I* like to say something." He turned to the prince. "We have been together much these last months and I know you well now—better than anyone except your wife. And so I know you do not really want to be king. You say so many times when we are alone together, and you say it again just now. You do not want to be king because you know what it means. All your life you have been pre-paring for it—studying, thinking—and still you do not want it. What you would like is to be private, be with your wife and son, teaching at university. On other hand, there is your stepbrother, Count John. He not only want to be king, he want it enough so that he kill for it! And what kind of king would he make? Not good—a very bad king! I say to you, men who do not really want to be kings are usually the ones who should be. And those who want to be—want it too much—are usually wrong. But whether you want it or not, I say you *should* be king! And so I ask you—no, I beg you in the name of your father and my father—that you not say no to it!"

The prince looked at him for a long moment and then at his wife.

"Well, my dear, what have you to say now?"

She did not look at him. She looked down, but Andrew had a feeling that she was looking inside herself.

"You asked me if I could accept the idea and what it means to me, to Michael, and to you," she said finally. "And the answer is, yes, I can. But the decision—the final decision as to whether you will or will not be king—must be yours."

"Yes, I suppose it must be," said the prince.

Now he looked at the three young people—and Andrew had a feeling that he was not just seeing them, but hundreds, thousands of other young people—everyone, in fact, who would help make up the future. Andrew had always been interested in history. And he suddenly had a sense that this was what it was about—what it *was*—not just dates, battles, laws, but what people thought and did about other people, the decisions no one knew about that changed the course of the world's affairs.

Finally the prince nodded. "All right, Mitya," he said. "I promise you that when the time comes, I won't say no."

Dimitroff let out his breath in a long sigh, and Andrew realized that he had been holding his breath, too.

"I don't think the pub's closed yet," said Chadwick. "But even if it is, do you think you can use your influence with the landlord, Wyatt? This calls for a toast—and one that can only be drunk in champagne."

"I couldn't agree with you more," said Wyatt.